I0587867

Also by V. A. Trahan

Graveyard of Metal

Tap Tap

V. A. Trahan

CVTrahan Publishing
Tioga, TX USA

This book is a work of fiction. Names, characters, places, and incidents are the product of the author's imagination or are used fictionally. Any resemblance to actual events, locales, or persons, living or dead, is coincidental.

Copyright © 2021 by

V. A. Trahan

All rights reserved. No part of this book may be reproduced or transmitted in any form by any means, electronic or mechanical, including photocopying, recording or by any information storage or retrieval system, without permission in writing from the copyright owner.

ISBN: 978-1-7369473-3-3

This book was published in the U.S.A. by CVTrahan Publishing

To my sons,

Marc Macione and Frank Mastrangelo

Finnegan's Wake

(Irish Ballad circa 1860)

Tim Finnegan lived in Walkin Street
A gentle Irishman, mighty odd
He'd a beautiful brogue so rich and sweet
And to rise in the world he carried a hod

You see he'd a sort of the tipp' lin' way
With the love of the liquor, poor Tim was born
And to help him on with his work each day
He'd a drop of the craythur every morn

One mornin' Tim was rather full
His head felt heavy, which made him shake
He fell from the ladder and he broke his skull
And they carried him home his corpse to wake

They rolled him up in a nice clean sheet
And laid him out upon the bed
With a gallon of whiskey at his feet
And a barrel of porter at his head

His friends assembled at the wake
And Mrs. Finnegan called for lunch
First they brought in tay and cake
Then pipes, tobacco and whiskey punch
Biddy O'Brien began to cry
"Such a nice clean corpse did you ever see?
Tim Mavourneen why did you die?"
"Arrah hold your gob" said Paddy McGee

Then Maggie O'Connor took up the job
"O Biddy, " says she "you're wrong I'm sure"
Biddy gave her a belt in the gob
And left her sprawling on the floor

Then the war did soon engage
It was woman to woman and man to man
Shillelagh law was all the rage
And a row and a ruction soon began

Then Mickey Maloney raised his head
When a bucket of whiskey flew at him
It missed and falling on the bed
The liquor scattered over Tim

Tim revives; see how he rises
Timothy rising from the bed
Said "Whirl your whiskey around like blazes
Thundering Jesus, do you think I'm dead?"

Dead End

Blackness... Pure night
      Dead end so bright
Alone I'll stay... Plagued with fright
      Don't go away... Where is the light?

Blank space... Stay strong
      Human race... Missed its song.

Don't go... Bestow to live and grow
      Born and die... High and low.

Be still, don't cry... Dark as night
      Low down deep... Lost my sight.

Don't fret... Don't weep
      This fight's for life... Less time to keep
No time for strife.
      Now try to sleep.

My rhythms gone? How will I know?
      Time feels so long... Where will I go?
I'll stay for now. My spirit's low
      Some way, somehow... I'll take it slow.

Please leave a sign for me today
      Grant one more breadth, so I can pray.

PROLOGUE

Every breadth... I try... To take is heavy. It's like my chest has been sat on by an elephant. I can breathe out only. I'll cry softly to myself. Exhale... Inhale... Now this is scary. I'm totally blind. I can't see or hear anything... Well maybe some things. Let me try. I'll put all myself, my strength, my everything into this feeling of un-living. Is that even a word? Am I fading away? Now I'm going to try to live. For what it's worth, I feel like I'm floating and scared.

Is this the end? My fingers won't move on command. I have no self strength on any part of my being anymore. My arm feels like it's just dangling in air, and I can't change that no matter how hard I try. I feel like I'm in a marathon, not to run, but to live.

Am I still sitting at my dining room table? I'm not totally sitting anymore. I believe I am flopped over or am I hanging off a chair. I keep trying, but I can't move. Will someone find me? I can't see my own finger. But I can feel it. I think. I can feel the nail is gone. Or is it? That's pain I feel. Wait... My foot has a bit of feeling. It's a charley horse. Wait... It's gone now. Come back cramp. Wait... I have consciousness. I must be alive.

Where am I? Am I still in my dining room? Did I eat my peanut butter sandwich? I'm not in pain at all. At least if I'm dying I guess I am just leaving. Where will I go? But I don't want to leave yet. Wait. This is really scary. I suddenly feel so out of control, and extremely out of sorts.

What if I just try harder? Maybe I should will myself and push my life back inside. I think it's trying to leave. So... Let me try. I don't want my life to end like this. Maybe I can squeeze just a bit of life back... Just a bit... Just enough.

Let me just review what I know right now... Mark was here, we kissed, we laughed, and we walked into the laundry room and talked.

He asked for a glass of water. I asked, 'Wouldn't you like coffee?'. What did he say? I think he said, 'No, water'. I walked into the kitchen and felt a bit dizzy. I sat down. I think he helped himself. He said I looked peaked and maybe I should have a glass of water myself. He was being kind. He brought me a glass of water and the newspaper.

We both sat at the kitchen table. I felt better. Or did I? He made me a peanut butter sandwich. Did I eat any of it? I wasn't dizzy anymore, or was I?

Sooo... Let me run through this one more time... After that, we both walked into the dining room. I brought my paper and sat and we chit chatted for a moment. But then I felt a bit light headed, again. I don't know for sure if I moved into the dining room or not. I believe I did. I think at that point I brought the sandwich with me. Or did Mark bring the sandwich? It doesn't matter, but I think I talked with confusion about a crossword puzzle word. What was a four letter word for dead? I think... I believed the answer was 'late'. Mark didn't know. I don't think Mark joined me in the dining room. I believe he was standing. I think he just stood there and looked at me with concern.

Mark said it would be better if he left and came back tomorrow, same time. Couldn't he tell something was wrong? There must have been signs. Didn't I look sick? But what did I say. I don't remember. What if there is no tomorrow. He left so quick... I think. Was he even here? I can't be sure of anything anymore.

So, then did I take a bite of my sandwich? There should be a lingering taste of peanut butter in my mouth. But it's not there. I think I drank my water. My mouth is so dry. Maybe I didn't. Wait... I wanted to drink my water... That's it, something was bothering me. I couldn't figure out how to get the glass up to my mouth... Maybe I just changed my mind?

Why did Mark leave? When did he leave? Was I so confused and maybe he didn't realize how serious my situation was?

There goes that charley horse again. My foot is still alive. I feel it. I'm not dead. I'm alive. Thank God. But I need to be taken to the hospital. They'll find out what's wrong with me there. I hate hospitals.

I can't feel my foot anymore now. I can't get a deep breath either. Why can't I inhale? Maybe I'm having a stroke. What in God's name is a stroke anyway? I think I read something about not having enough oxygen to the brain. Brain cells start to die without oxygen. So have some of my brain cells died? God, I hope not.

Maybe I'm dead and this is the way it feels to die. You don't really go unconscious; you just go into another dimension. And you don't have any jurisdiction of your being. Okay then no control, but I feel alive. I must be in that other dimension where I can't control myself anymore. I believe my brain is still percolating though. I don't think I want to float around aimlessly like a balloon. I don't think, but I can think. I can't talk.

But... Oh no... What about love? I won't have that warmth anymore either. Oh God. I've had a sharp tongue in the past. I don't know how to change that. What will happen now? I'm so sorry. I know, I know... I should have apologized to them. You know those that maybe I belittled or criticized in the past. I now will atone for any bad behavior if you give me one more chance.

This is getting too scary. This time I'm going to ask you to help me figure out what's going on. I know I have an oxygen deprived brain. That's not good. I need plenty of oxygen. Please give me... Just enough. I know some of my brain cells are functional. Give me a sign. Let me know if I'm gone. Anything, just a token maybe... Give me my sight back. Or let me scream something or just a small amount of sound...

My foot had feeling... Maybe give me back that charley horse. It hurt but pain can be a good thing. It will let me know I'm alive and not dead. If I can hear, I think that would be good.

Is that my dog? Do I hear you Finnegan? Are you crying? I feel you're close... Finnegan! You're here with me, aren't you boy? Am I right? Help your mommy. I can't see you. I can't talk. I sense you're here though. I love you... Wait... Is this a sign? Maybe it is. You're the best dog. I still have love. Do something to let me know I'm alive. Lick my face or bark... Just something. But don't leave. Please help me Finney. Come here boy. Wait... I can't feel or sense you're here... I'm alive aren't I? Is that all there is? That's okay then, that's just enough. Wait... What's happening?

April 13, 8:30 a.m.

It was a crisp, sunny, spring morning in Bucks County, Pennsylvania. Buds and blooms were on the trees and shrubs everywhere. The road workers were filling pot holes with pea gravel. This was a time for rebirth, a promise of a new day. The temperature was expected to be warming up for the next two days. New flowers were popping up in the fields, like wild day lilies and daffodils. Folks were ready to be out and about at the parks and walking on the sidewalks again, getting fresh air, after a long exceptionally cold winter.

Carol Rose was heading to the Christmas sale at the Peddler's Village in Bucks County. It was April thirteenth and nobody was thinking of Christmas in April. Or at least most people don't. Especially when the weather was particularly warm, but those clever bargain hunters do. That was why an early annual sale was always a big deal. It was advertized in the local County Messenger, in Krum, PA. The sale was to continue through June first, but by two p.m. April thirteenth all the great buys were usually gone, done, and kaput. Sure there would still be sale items, but not like the first five hours.

She was focusing on specific antique toys for her granddaughter Kellie. Carol used to bring Kellie when she was younger because they had a train set there that went from the first booth of the flea market display, through to the other end of the building. The display ended with a silly clown that gave out taffies and candy canes. The kids all loved it. Carol never liked the looks of the clown though. She thought he was hideous and wouldn't let Kellie sit on his lap. Instead Carol would buy a treat for Kellie in lieu of the candy the clown gave out.

Carol lived next door to the cemetery and across the street from Pat. She had a clear view of Pat's comings and goings. She'd been thinking of reconciling with her once best friend.

She noticed this morning there was a pile of building material on the side of Pat's driveway. She also remembered seeing Mark's white truck leave an hour ago. It had been there for no more than a half hour. She knew Mark was an expert carpenter and he was considered one of the finer craftsmen/handymen in town and wondered what construction, what changes, were going on at Pat's house.

She was anxious to find out the answer to the question; was Pat really having work done?

She noticed that Pat was slimmer than ever and her once sandy brown hair was now more of a ash blonde color. She had lost some weight and was looking very pretty in recent days, ever since she had been having all her carpentry work completed. She also seemed to be seeing quite a bit more of Mark on a more social setting. Carol's curiosity was getting the best of her.

Blink... Blink! A light bulb lit in Carol's brain and she said out loud as she was driving down her road, "Pat you would love this sale."

As she turned her car around at the cemetery driveway to backtrack over to Pat Faros' house, she noticed all the buds on the trees. "This should be a sign of new beginnings," she whispered. She was tired of having bad karma with her special 'across the street neighbor'. Even though they haven't spoken for almost a year now she was hoping that time had worn away the kink in their relationship. She was hoping this would put the brakes on their previous disagreements.

She said out loud, "I always meant well Pat. "

She found herself feeling strangely nervous for some reason as she parked her car on Pat's newly paved driveway. Carol scouted the walkway and carefully watched her step due to a recent injury to her left knee that had caused her to use a cane to get around easier. She paced herself slowly until she reached Pat's front door.

At first she found herself standing in a cowering position. "I'm going to jump in with both feet, although one might be a bit sore," she said softly to herself. "What am I going to say to her?"

Pat's Antique blue door grabbed her attention, it had been freshly painted. She thought, *How lovely*. She knocked a bit timidly. No answer. She then used her car key to knock on the small peek-a-boo window on top of the door, hoping not to lose her balance. Pat didn't answer. She hadn't seen Pat leave today.

"Hmmm... "

Carol knew her comings and goings and she believed she should be home. Living across the street offered Carol great spying advantage.

Finnegan the poodle barked frantically. She looked through the large picture window into the living room in front of the house. Pat usually looked out that window before she would answer the door. Carol knocked again. This time she wanted to see if Pat was hiding from her. That was a possibility. Maybe she just didn't want to see her.

She tried to reach the window but had to climb across Pat's freshly planted flower bed. This was a daunting task with her cane. Carol carefully crossed over the new spring plants accidentally injuring one of the new sprouts.

"Oh no, Pat I'm sorry!" She bent down holding her cane and pushed the pansy back into the ground. She pulled herself up a bit off balance and peeked through the window. *What do I see,* she thought? The glare of the sun caused her to squint. *What am I looking at?*

Right at that moment the reflection off the window caused her a moment of pause. Then she blinked to get a better view of what she thought she was looking at. She could see Pat lying halfway on and halfway off a chair at her dining room table. She wasn't moving. Her head was near the floor her arm straight out like maybe she was trying to catch herself. But one thing was for sure, she was lying there limp, and not moving. She looked like she needed immediate help.

Carol called, "Pat... Yoo-hoo... It's me Carol. Something is very wrong here. Are you okay?"

Carol tapped with her keys on the window attempting to get Pat's attention. Finnegan continued barking and ran to the picture window looking at Carol. But there was no response from Pat. Carol with her eagle perfect eyesight examined the surroundings. She looked at the complete landscape of Pat's side yard. She searched around at the cemetery entrance, across the street. She then examined the other side of Pat's, at Mr. Powell's house. She couldn't see anyone, anywhere.

She limped over to the door and played with the door knob. She turned, pushed and pulled frantically. No question, it was locked. She looked under the front door mat for a possible key. No luck. She scrambled around to the back of the house, cane in tow. That door was locked also.

She pulled her cell phone out of her shoulder strap purse. Despite her injured leg she sprinted to the front of the house. She looked one last time through the window then yelled, "Pat it's me Carol," She knocked loud and called, "Pat!" No response. She quickly phoned May, Pat's daughter.

May, who was in the middle of a grocery shop at Safe Saver, attempted to answer her phone that was on a loud ring tone. She stared at it for a moment before she picked it up quickly. Her husband Dan often called several times a day and her phone rang so much she recently had to change her ring tone. It used to be Woody Woodpecker. Her daughter Michelle put that on her phone, for fun. It was so embarrassing whenever she received a phone call in public. The new tone was a bit more acceptable. She was used to receiving calls at an inopportune time.

May answered ready to pounce on her husband with words. "Dan what is it *this* time?" There was a slight pause. "Hello!" Then there was a moment of silence. Then there was... No response at all. "Hello!"

Carol dropped her phone, but managed to pick it up without falling. She then blurted out, "May this is Carol, I'm calling about your mother. She's in her house looking like she needs help."

"What? Carol what do you mean she needs help?"

"I'm at her house looking through her picture window and I can see she is lying halfway on and halfway off her dining room chair. I can see her clearly. She is hanging down like she had fainted or something. I believe she needs emergency help!"

"What? Carol, go in her house! See if you can help her! I'll be right there!"

"The door is locked!"

"Carol... Call 911!"

Carol hung up and tried the door again. She thought to herself, *Why am I wasting time, it's definitely locked.* She proceeded to dial 911.

Carol informed 911 that she had attempted to open the door but it was locked. She also said Pat was not responding to loud rapping on her door and her dog was barking frantically.

She told them, "I could see looking through her window she was hanging off her chair." Lastly she told them Pat's daughter was on her way.

May pulled up at her mother's house, beating the ambulance. She jumped out of her car and immediately unlocked the front door.

Carol apologetically blurted out, "May, I tried the back door too, but *it* was locked."

Carol followed May into the house. Finnegan greeted them barking and jumping around like a pogo stick. May caught a glimpse of her mother in the dining room and called, "Mommy!" Finnegan jumped up on May. "Get down Finney!"

May let out a scream, "Mommy... No please... No don't go! Oh my God! She's gone! Carol, I think she's gone!" She stood at the dining room entrance way.

May held her mother's wrist to check for a pulse. She couldn't find one. She screamed, "Carol should I lay her on the floor?"

Sirens and voices could be heard at the front of Pat's house.

"No, the emergency team is here! They will do that."

May peered at her mother in such an awkward position. May felt helpless and the fear on her face was evident. "What should I do Carol, I don't know what to do?"

Carol shook her head "Move out of the way honey. The emergency team is coming in now."

Carol said with assurance, "May, your mom will be in good hands. She'll be fine. She needs their emergency care. We can only pray they can help her. I'll stay with you dear; just stay clear and out of their way."

May touched her mother's extended arm with her hand one more time. She jerked her hand back quickly and said, "No, Oh my God... Mommy, don't you dare die!"

May began heaving, and then there was wailing. Not crying, she was simply shrieking, and howling, like a mournful lone animal.

Carol grabbed hold of May and tried to soothe her pain. She held her close, and rocked her. "Calm down sweetie, I know this is rough, she'll be in good hands."

Pat's head was almost on the floor now. Her left arm was over her head and her right arm was straight up like she was attempting to get up. But her face was a pale grey. Her arm was stiff and cold to the touch.

May stared, studying the position her mother was in, and then mumbled, "What happened to you Mommy? Please don't go. "

The emergency crew rushed into the house. Carol waved and directed them to where Pat was. They quickly pulled Pat down onto the carpeted floor and started CPR.

The unit of three attendants, one woman and two men, worked on Pat with expert, immediate, medical care.

Carol briefed the emergency crew giving them a quick update of what and when she noticed Pat needed help.

May handed the older attendant a list of her medications that she takes. They quickly put Pat on to a stretcher. Her arms were now along her sides. They continued CPR. The litter was brought around and she was slipped onto the gurney like putty. They left with Pat on the stretcher. In a flash they were gone. May stood watching every move of the emergency crew, her hands holding her face. Her eyes filled with tears. This was really happening! All May could say now was, "No don't go Mommy! No please Mommy!"

May wiped her tear covered face with the back of her hand and hollered to the ambulance driver, "Should I ride with her?"

The female attendant shook her head. "Sorry, we don't have room; we're going to do everything we can to attempt to keep her alive."

"Okay, I'll meet you guys at the hospital." The tall, 'in charge' looking older man acknowledged her comment, and they left.

Finnegan came running and barking at the emergency vehicle, but he was too late. They'd gone already. He attempted to protest them taking his owner away. He cry barked with some whining added. He sniffed under the dining table where a trace of DNA might have been left of his mommy. Finnegan sadly hunkered down under the table. He heaved a big sigh and then fell asleep.

Carol propped her cane against the sofa and embraced May in her arms. "It's scary to have this happen May,"

Carol said. She patted May on the back and said, "Come on I'll drive you."

Carol held her cane tight and walked with May to her car feeling quite a bit of pain from all the running. May hopped into Carol's car and they headed to Krum General Hospital outside of Plum City. Carol suffered with double pain but she was determined to stay with her friend's daughter through this tragedy. They noticed the emergency parking lot was full and had to use the garage parking. Carol said it looked busy today.

May called her uncle, Frank, on her cell phone as they hurried through the parking garage. Pat's brother Frank was instructed to inform family members of the medical emergency and that Pat was already at the hospital.

Frank tried to alleviate the stress that he heard in May's voice. "May, she'll be fine. Listen May, she isn't going to die. She's too ornery. You know that. This could be anything. She may have just passed out."

May sobbed, "But I saw her face, Uncle Frank. She looked dead and she felt cold to the touch. She might have been there for a while. I think she's dead. I don't know. We might have been too late."

"May, Sweetie, wait! I'll meet you at the hospital. Wait until you talk to someone. After you talk to a trained medical person they will explain how your mother is doing. Don't think those negative thoughts."

May began crying uncontrollably, "I'm walking into the hospital right now. Oh my God, I'll call you back. Pray for her Uncle."

"May, hold on girl, I'll be right there."

April 13, 10:00 a.m.

As Carol limped her way through the long hospital corridor, she waved May on in, to get a head start. May needed to find out how her mother was progressing. She pulled her mother's emergency cards out of her pocket book. She had Xerox copied health cards. She had copies of her mother's medications and a copy of her driver's license. She kept them in her purse in case they were needed, for situations just like this. Her mother was diagnosed with breast cancer six years ago and May had the responsibility of taking care of Pat, so she was prepared. She kept a copy of her mother's cards in her own wallet.

May wanted to walk back now and visit with her mother. She was very anxious to find out how her mother was progressing. But she was stopped by the head nurse in the emergency department who held her hand up in a commanding manner.

She said, "Stop right there... From going any further. That's as far as you can go dear. I'll call you. They continue working on Mrs. Faros at this time. So sit tight. I realize this is stressful, but I know where to find you."

May continued sobbing and sniffling as she turned and looked for Carol. She fast walked in her direction. She recognized that Carol was limping more noticeably. May said she would scout out the waiting room and find a couple of seats together. The emergency room seemed to be bustling with people. Every seat was taken.

Carol and May began walking. They looped around the large waiting room full of family members, meticulously scrutinizing the room for a couple of seats.

"How could it be this crowded?" Carol said with a bit of sarcasm, "Is everybody that lives in this town sick or visiting someone at the hospital? I can't believe it."

Carol was exhibiting quite a bit of pain by now. They continued their slow shuffle along looking for a place to sit together. Both sobbing and inching their way as slow as a caterpillar. May held onto Carol when she seemed to miss a step.

"Oops!"

They began walking with more intention in their step. They continued at a slow but steady pace. They were waiting for the triage nurse to direct them at any moment.

"What could have happened? I don't get it Carol. She was fine when I called her this morning!" May cried looking for an answer. "Carol, she took vitamins. She ate oatmeal and blueberries every day. She was healthier than me! She was exercising a couple days a week. She was just starting to explore life from a new perspective. She was cancer free. That's a biggie. She was going out, once in a while. She just turned sixty-five. That's still young, in the senior world. What could have happened to her? I guess its genetics. She did say her mother, my Nan, died at sixty-five. She said that she wouldn't make it past sixty-five."

Carol looked over at May. "She was in very good shape. I heard she was joining pickle ball too."

May bug eyed stared at Carol, "Really, pickle ball? I didn't know that. Where?"

"At the community center, I think. Didn't she teach an art class for seniors there once? They just started a pickle ball group there. She and Mark signed up. Now that's second hand news from Nancy Davis. Nancy seemed to know everything. Maybe she was just talking about it. But Pat is young at heart. That would be good for her. I know she's been looking better than ever lately."

They both scoped out the waiting room while they paced their steps around each seat. They were sobbing and sniffling. Carol with her cane and an extra pause in her limp. They were getting tired of walking when they noticed a couple that appeared to be getting ready to leave.

May said, "I always think the worst, in these situations. What if she dies? Oh darn... Look at me I'm a mess. Maybe she'll be fine. I shouldn't be so negative and think more positive thoughts like Uncle Frank said."

Carol nodded and said, "Yes, think positive today. I'll try and help by doing the same."

"Carol, what happened to you? Why the cane? You look like you're in pain."

"I am right now. I fell in the grocery store; you know that deli food store, Rocky's? I guess he had just washed the floor. I barely took one step and slipped. I landed on my knee. So I injured my patella, in my knee cap."

May made a scrunched up face, "Oh my, that must have hurt, and you do look like you're in quite a bit of pain right now."

"I am. But I'll be fine. The cane helps and I get around okay. At least I don't need surgery at this time. It's nothing too serious sweetie. Just fluid that builds up in the knee from the injury.

"You know that mom and pop grocery store on Main Street; it's a block from the hospital? Well, I lay on the floor for several minutes before that gnarly old guy, Rocky himself said, 'What did you do... Walk on the wet floor?' He pulled me up like a sack of potatoes, kind of like I did something wrong and then he walked away. It really hurt at the time, my feelings as much as the fall. Up until then he was always nice to me. I don't know why he was so rude that day."

May smirked and looked away. "I would sue his butt. I've met him outside of the store. He lives a block away from me. I just wave to him. He waves back. But he sounds like a grump to me. At least, he wouldn't be getting my business anymore. Who does he think he is?"

Carol said, "I've been in the store since, but I don't chit-chat with him, even when he talks about his son. Anthony and I were in several classes in high school together way back when. He never once asked me how my leg was. I just get my change and off I go. He has the best lunch meat around though, and his rolls are always so fresh. I would have to drive too far to avoid his store."

Carol stopped walking when she heard a ding that came from her cell phone. She had a message from a guy she referred to as her 'dinner buddy'. Bill was a widower that was just looking for 'date night' fun. He's sixty-five and recently retired with tons of money. Which made Carol quite pleased? Carol texted, *I will call you later.*

May said aloud, "Carol, over there, two seats." She pointed at the seats side by side in the corner. They shuffled their way over to the comfortable seats and planted themselves while waiting for the latest revelation from the nurse. Carol plopped down and grimaced in pain. With both her hands Carol began rubbing her very sore knee. It was swollen now. She said, "Owww!"

May wept softly, "This just can't be happening; she just went to the doctors. She had her annual physical and she had high cholesterol; she's been on a statin prescription to control it. I read somewhere that statins can contribute to brain bleeds. So let's hope that's not the case."

She sobbed, looked over at Carol, and said, "I just spoke to her this morning. She was working on her crossword puzzle. She needed a three letter word that meant poke. I couldn't think of an answer. I told her I just called to invite her to go to a dinner theater to see 'Girls are from Venus, Men are from Mars'. It's playing at the Peddler's Dinner Theater. I heard it was very funny. I was going with two of my friends for a girl's night out. She would have loved that. The girls have so much fun. She's been a bit bored lately. Or at least I thought she was. She keeps me guessing.

"Anyway, I told her I had a surprise for her and was going to get her a ticket, but she wouldn't have it. She had her mind set on asking Mark, that handyman guy, who's putting up those darn shelves in her laundry room... That job seems to be taking forever, anyway, we wanted to take Mom with us. But she was going to ask Mark to go with her instead.

"What a disappointment. It would have been so much fun. Mom is so much fun to go out with. But I do understand. Who knows, maybe she's in love with him."

As Carol continued to rub her leg she looked over at May and said, "The word for the crossword puzzle was possibly 'jab'."

"Yep, you're right! My brain can't do two things at once anymore. Mom and I race to try to finish the crossword puzzle every morning. It's a daily game we play together. She usually wins though. She's really my best friend Carol. I don't know what I'd do if she died." May sniffled again.

"Let me tell you why I went over to her house. I was getting brave enough to have a truce with your mother. I've missed her so much. I was hoping she would forgive me for my bad behavior.

"I was going to ask her to join me at the spring Christmas sale at Peddler's Village. Today was the first day, which is the best day to go. Anyway, they have

Christmas style gifts and ornaments, and lots of other gift type items. Anyway, for the first five hours you can make a killing. After that you can still find good deals and beautiful items cheaper than you can find them during the Christmas holidays. But your best bet is nine a.m. April thirteenth. The sale lasts until June first. I was just hoping she would have forgiven me."

May nodded her head. "She would have. She told me not too long ago she missed you. Now I remember. She would have forgiven you for that stunt concerning Finnegan. She's just been so mesmerized with Mark she can't think of anything else. I think she's actually in love with him. He sent her beautiful flowers at her birthday party. Were you there?"

"Oh, yes. I wouldn't have missed it. I don't think she would have invited me. Michelle, your daughter, handed me an invitation. But, Pat smiled at me at the party. She said 'Hi!', and didn't ignore me. That was promising. But she didn't have a conversation with me like she normally would have when things were better between us.

"However, I didn't wear a costume. Maybe she would have had a friendlier disposition if I were a vampire. Who knows? Anyway, I saw the two love birds, stuck together like glue. Those flowers Pat received were beautiful. They were roses. That's the love sign you know. He's taken with her. Your mom deserves to find someone like

Mark that she can enjoy to do things with. Oh, and by the way, he's a cutie pie."

"Do you think I should call Mark? After all he was the last one to see her, you said."

"Well, let's not speculate. Let's see what they say about your mother first."

"Oh, okay."

Carol shook her head, "Not yet anyway. This could be a long day May. I'll call him later for you."

Without warning, Doctor Landrum came striding into the waiting room; almost a run. He was looking for May Burns. He looked around and announced, "May Burns?" He scouted out the room and spotted May. He looked right into her eyes; like he was clairvoyant, He said, "Are you May Burns?"

May nodded her head, stunned that the doctor recognized her. She was frightened to hear anything else. What was he going to say? She returned the stare, but with a bit of fear in her eyes. "That's me!" She stood up too quick and a dizzy feeling swept over her. "Yes?"

"Hi, my name is Dr. Landrum and... I would like you to join me in that room over there." He pointed toward the Sanctuary.

He was young but he had an authoritative look, and a commanding voice. He walked ahead of May and pointed to the small room. Carol stood up watching May follow the doctor. She squeezed a tight hold onto an empty chair in front of her and with her other hand she readied her cane against her leg.

May followed close behind the doctor and said with anxiety in her voice, "Why, is she dead?"

Dr. Landrum slowly turned toward the Sanctuary and signaled with his eyes for May to follow him. As he ushered her in with a methodically slow pace she began sobbing. He does not address her question.

"Come with me May."

When she walked into the room Dr. Landrum pulled the door shut.

Frank, Pat's brother, dashed into the waiting room, just missing his niece. He recognized Carol and flagged her with a hand wave. She was still standing next to her chair with her mouth wide open.

He called to Carol, "Hi Carol, is everything alright?"

She closed her mouth and stared into Frank's eyes. "Oh. Hello Frank. May is in the Sanctuary talking to the doctor."

Frank asked, "Is Pat okay?"

Carol pointed toward the room and said, "The doctor is informing May right now, I'm praying she's okay but..."

Frank wrapped his hands around his face, trying to hold back his tears. "She's always been my rock, she can't die. I don't know what I'd do without her." He said a silent prayer.

Carol and Frank both stood facing the small closed door to the Chapel. The people that were sitting near were now gawking at Carol and Frank. May's pocketbook was left wide open on the chair. Her cell phone began ringing to the tune of Blackbird, by The Beatles. They were standing waiting for a signal from May. Carol held onto the back of an empty seat. Her fingers began sweating. She ignored the musical tune as May's cell phone continued to ring.

Frank looked at Carol. "She'll probably be fine. But maybe her cancer is back. That wouldn't be too good. He shook his head. What am I saying... God I hope she'll be okay?"

Carol replied, "I don't think so Frank. Remember, I found her. She didn't look like she was going to make it to me."

He scratched his head and turned facing the small room. "This can't be happening. God please help her."

The two peered at the door of the sanctuary for many minutes that seemed like an hour. Some of the surrounding folks that were eavesdropping were also watching the door. Suddenly, out of the small room came a horrid resounding message from May. She bellowed, "Nooo!" It could be heard by everyone in the room. One woman sitting across from them made the sign of the cross.

May came out of the Sanctuary and called Carol and Frank to join her. She was blowing her nose and crying softly. Carol picked up her purse and May's pocket book as the phone continued the Beatles melody. Frank helped with the two pocket books while Carol steadied her cane.

In the Sanctuary there was a pretty stained glass window and a kneeling hassock on the floor. There were two benches and four maple wooden chairs with colorful cushioned seats. When the door was closed it was quite soothing. The light streamed in through the scalloped windows and the room was dim and quiet.

May and Frank sat on a chair side by side in the room. Carol put Mays pocket book on one of the empty chairs. May's phone rang again. May was able to answer the call. It was her daughter. "Hello, Michelle. Nan is gone. She died honey! ... I know, I know. I won't be too long. ... I Love you too. Say a prayer for Nan."

Frank picked up his cell phone and called his wife Kathryn quietly telling her the devastating news. He attempted to call Bo but when it went to voice mail he left a message to call his mother ASAP.

They all began crying and Carol patted Frank on his back. "She was a wonderful person. I was just going to spend the day with her," Carol said with pure sorrow in her voice.

May hung up after speaking with her daughter. She began crying again. "She loved her Nan." Uncle Frank and May hugged and cried together. Carol cried quietly at her seat. A priest stepped inside the room.

"Hello, my name is Father Michael from St. Joseph's across the street from the hospital. I understand that your loved one Patricia Faros has passed away today. I stayed by her side when she arrived. I believe she died peacefully but she had already been pronounced dead when I arrived at her side. First I want to offer my deepest sympathy."

He looked at May and said, "I want to add that I just left your mother. I am a Eucharist Minister. I was able to give her the last rites. She was not conscious, she was already gone, but in Jesus name I believe she was aware I was there. Your mother has passed out of this world and is on the long journey to the next, to be with the Lord God in Heaven."

They all made the sign of the cross and said the Our Father. May began sobbing and the priest put his hand on her forehead and prayed for spiritual strength. Then they all said the rosary together.

Father Michael gave a blessing to everyone in the Sanctuary and left.

Within minutes, a social worker knocked on the door and came in slowly. She looked for May. "May, my name is Gloria Donohue. I want to offer my deepest sympathy to you and your family." May acknowledged her condolence.

"This is a tough time in your life but each day will feel better. Your memories hopefully will give you strength. I assure you that the sadness that you feel will ease with time. Right now you need your family. They are the only people that can give you peace."

She sat with the family for several minutes and then asked them if they had any questions. "What can I get any or all of you to drink? A glass of water, Soda, Juice?"

The girls asked for water and Frank sniffled. When he asked, "How about a black coffee?" Gloria said, "Certainly! I'll be right back." Then with a slight smile she quietly left.

April 13, 12:30 p.m.

Carol hugged Frank and May one last time. She said she would be home for the rest of the evening in case they needed her for anything.

Frank gave Carol the tentative funeral plan. Kathryn, Frank's wife, had just texted him the particulars for the morning. It was to be tomorrow; an open casket for one hour, 11:00 a.m. to noon, and then outside for the funeral and burial at 12:30, April fourteenth, the same day.

May thanked Carol for finding her mother in distress and alerting her. She thanked her for driving her to the hospital and staying with her at the hospital the whole time. Frank informed Carol he would take care of May now and drive her home. In pain and sorrow Carol left, slowly limping toward the exit.

May and Frank were led by the nurse in charge. The trio walked down to the bottom floor to the morgue. The temperature was a bit chilly down there. They noticed that two attendants were about to put Pat in one of those ice cold drawers. Frank stopped them and asked if they had signed off on the body yet. He handed them a directive that informed them there would not be organ donation from his sister's body. And someone from the funeral home was already on their way to pick her up. While they waited for Blain, the funeral director, who happened to know Frank very well, they wanted to stay with Pat to talk with her.

May was given a chair to sit on while Frank looked at Pat and spoke softly to her, "Sis, you've always been there for me. I'll think of you when I see my son Bo. You will be my inspiration to be a better person. I love you. Say hello to Mom and Dad and Martha. God Bless you. You were the sunshine in my life. Thank you so much for being you, Sis. I'll see you in the next life." He began sobbing.

May cradled her face crying softly. "Tell Mommy I love her. I need a moment before I have the nerve to see her. I can't look at her right now for some reason. I'm so afraid. It's like I'm in a nightmare."

~

Brrr, why am I so cold? I can hear you guys talking. I can't seem to respond. Hello... Can anybody hear me? I guess not. Where am I? I am freezing! Did I hear something? May? Frank? Where in God's name am I?

Frank, what do you mean, 'I'll see you in the next life'? Take care of this life now, and see they rescue me. I'm not dead!

I feel a strong draft of cold air. I feel so cold, I am definitely alive. Damn! I'm in a hospital... I think.

Frank, stop you're sobbing and help me. I've never seen you cry like a baby. Very sweet, but now just stop and let's take care of business. They do know I'm not dead, right?

~

May finally made up her mind. She was going to look at her mother. She walked over to her cautiously, sniffling. She now began crying hard.

"Why, Mom? Why did you die before Michelle's prom and her graduation?" Her sobbing continued. "How can I face her? She wanted you to see her in the dress you made her. Mommy, you don't look dead. What happened to you anyway?"

~

I heard you May. Why are you crying? I'm not really dead. I don't think they pronounced me deceased, or did they?

What's this about Michelle's prom and graduation? So you think I'm dead, do you... How can you talk about Michelle's prom and the dress I made her. And ask, 'Why did you die before her graduation?' Is that the first thing you think about when your mother dies? Or at least you think I'm dead.

May, get me outta here! I'm not dead. Why can't you hear me? I'm just not able to speak. I can't see you. I'm trying... Humph.

I can hear you though. Stop the sniffling, crying and help me. All you can think about is Michelle's prom and graduation? May, I'm in kind of a predicament. You've got to help me. Good Grief girl!

~

"Hello you two. My name's Jeremy and I was told your mother..." He looked at May. He then turned and looked at Frank, "...and your sister, have passed. I'm so very sorry for your loss. You both have suffered a devastating loss of your loved one. Because we care, we are going to put your loved one in cold storage. You know, one of those drawers over there. That will keep your loved one refrigerated, fresh and crisp."

~

Wait... Fresh and crisp... What am I a head of lettuce? Don't you dare put me in a refrigerator drawer! I'm already fresh. Can you cover me with a warm blanket instead... Please? I'm getting frozen. I'm going to turn into an icicle soon. Come on, I'd rather wilt than freeze.

~

Jeremy points to the mortuary drawers. "She'll stay nice and cold that way. That is when you're finished visiting with her. Okay?"

Frank stared at Pat and said, "She wanted to go directly to the funeral home from the hospital. That was her strict request. She didn't want her body to be cold."

Jeremy smiled and said, "She won't feel a thing. I assure you."

"We've already made arrangements for my sister to be immediately sent to Deer Path Funeral Home. Her funeral will be tomorrow. Her announcement was already prepared and sent by my wife Kathryn to specific relatives. She wanted it quick and simple."

Suddenly the back door opened. It was father and son, Bernard and Blain Smith. They arrived to pick up the body. When they walked into the room they brought a stretcher and a body cover; not a body bag. They walked over to the mortuary attendant and filled out the appropriate paperwork. May showed her identification and handed it to Jeremy so the body could be released. She had power of attorney over her mother's estate when her mother was not able to make decisions on her own. She was also the executor of her mother's will. Jeremy filled out a couple more papers and then May received from Jeremy a death registration pronouncement. She looked it over; it read cause of death embolic stroke.

Right then, nothing seemed real to May. She stood staring at her mother laying on the gurney looking so peaceful. May felt like she was floating; like this was just a dream, or was it real? Something was off. May felt a visceral affect. Something was just not quite right. This is just not happening. Her mind played a game with her. Mommy looked like she was simply asleep. May's subconscious seemed to be forcing her to believe she was still very much alive. May had to force herself to go through the rituals over a dead body. Her mother's death had somehow changed her. She was now the matriarch of her family. She now had to make important decisions.

"Mommy, why did you have to go and die? Now I have to make all these big decisions?"

~

Oh May, you poor, poor thing. I'm so sorry. Have I inconvenienced you? Why did I have to die? What a question. You've got to be kidding. By the way, I'm not dead!

~

May cried, "Mommy you poor thing. So that's what caused your sudden death." But she didn't feel she was talking to a dead person, "You poor, poor thing. You had an embolic stroke. I wish I could fix it."

~

A stroke, huh? So that's what's causing my confusion. What do you mean 'poor thing' Miss May? And you definitely can fix it. I'm a poor thing because nobody understands that I'm not dead! They made a big mistake. They're taking me somewhere. Where are they taking me, May?

Wait! Oh my God! They're taking me to a funeral home, aren't they? May, don't let them take me there. And... By the way, there was no sudden death, hence, I'm not dead. Just put on your thinking cap. Check my pulse. I need to stay at this hospital where sick people go; not a mortuary where dead people go. Somebody help me!

~

Blain and Bernard offered their condolences and quickly lifted Pat onto the stretcher, covered her from head to toe with a body blanket, and left in a black, shiny mini-van. Frank and May followed behind in Frank's brand new black truck. It felt like a funeral procession.

As Frank and May followed behind the mini-van they didn't talk. They sniffled a bit but nothing was said for just about the whole ride to the funeral home.

The funeral home was nestled at the end of the road of Deer Park Cemetery. They pulled up at the magnificent white stucco and stone home. May was struck by the beauty and grandeur of the home and surrounding perfectly manicured grounds. It afforded a peaceful backdrop for a painful event. They pulled onto the parking lot.

Frank looked questioningly at May, "Are you going to be able to do this? Are you going to be able to touch your mother? Can you makeup your mother with some cosmetics and maybe a nice hairdo?"

"Her hair is fine."

"Will you be able to fix her makeup or do you want Aunt Kathryn to do it?"

"No... I'll be okay. Do they supply the cosmetics?"

"Yes dear, they do. I believe they do anyway. But I'll ask. I'm not sure. Kathryn is here already. We can ask her."

As they looked around at the undertakers magnificent home they were now getting nervous. Kathryn had already arrived as she was designated to help with the arrangements. The floral bouquet scent was overly done but it smelled just like they imagined it would. It was starting to feel real to them now.

They quickly moved Pat into a backroom, through the showroom. As they carried Pat through the showroom the flowery scent was strong in the air. They moved into the back prep room for embalming or for makeup and hair. This is where one would get to work on their beloved family member.

The beautiful casket had been dropped off by Bo, who was waiting for everyone inside the back prep room. May slowly followed behind the trail of family members through to where Bo was sitting on a chair sobbing.

When the body was delivered onto the large makeup table, May stood staring with worrisome consternation. "I'm not sure I can do this," she said. "I'll try."

Aunt Kathryn had a hold on her with a firm grip, hoping she wouldn't faint.

"I'll help you May. I brought my own makeup just for this occasion. You won't have to use theirs." Kathryn was like a big sister to May. She protected her whenever the need came up.

Bernard pulled the cover off of Pat and she looked almost like she was alive.

"She looks good."

May walked over to her mother and petted her very gently. "Mommy, I'm going to try and make you look prettier than you do right now. I'm sorry if I don't do a good job. You are already so pretty. Look at her Kathryn. She doesn't look dead, does she?"

Kathryn stared for a moment and then shook her head. She laid out several colors of makeup, eyebrow pencil, rouge and lipstick.

~

May... Sweetie, it's your momma. Please don't put heavy makeup on me. Look dear girl... I'm not dead. Where in God's name am I?

Finnegan... Where's Finnegan? He's probably, by now, pooping in the laundry room. May, please go and take care of Finnegan.

I was in a hospital, now where am I? It smells like a funeral home. Just great! Now they're going to embalm me... Embalm! Oh God no, don't embalm me! I want to go, not now of course, but when it's time...ahhh...na-tu-ar-al.

Where are my clothes? I'm very modest. What do I feel. I feel a draft. I think... Or is it? I hope I'm dressed.

Don't put too much makeup on me girls. Even if I was dead, I don't want to look like a trollop.

~

"Before we do that," Blain said, "Bernard will have the body washed for the family."

They decided to move out of the immediate area and give the funeral director some privacy and space.

"This room is normally an embalming room."

Kathryn, who was a registered nurse, said she would stay with Pat's body during the washing. She was concerned and wanted to make sure they show her respect. She was given a plastic gown to wear and shoe coverings. Some folks wore masks and gloves for protection from bodily fluids. Kathryn chose not to wear a mask.

Bernard said, "Lets wash the body completely first. We'll go top to bottom with a strong detergent."

~

Whoa... Whoa... Whoa! Who in the world are you? This is not washing someone's dishes. Who in the world is he?

Kathryn, don't let him touch me! I don't recognize that voice. And why is he so concerned about using detergent?

~

"Do you want me to help", Kathryn said with careful concern.

"I assumed you wanted to help. You don't have to. But that is a normal procedure."

~

Wait one dang gone minute. That man, whoever he is, is NOT washing my body. Kathryn, you can wash me. But... Whoever that guy is, don't let him near me. Kathryn you are the one designated to wash me. Am I naked? Who is that guy?

~

Pat's body was lying on a stainless steel table. It had a head block that offered a variety of angles to properly wash all crevices of the body. May requested that Pat's hair *not* be washed as her mother had just been to the hairdresser the day before and the hairdo was especially styled the way Pat liked it. Her hair looked perfect May said and Bernard agreed.

~

Wait one minute! My neck feels sore now. I guess I feel a bit of a pinched pain. So don't hurt me. You're up to something. What's going on? I'm feeling cold air too. Am I naked now, or not?

~

Bernard told Kathryn, "The hospital left her hospital gown on her. You can remove the gown or leave it on."

Kathryn said, "Bernard, however you're accustomed to preparing the cadaver would be fine. I'll just take that gown off of her. *"*

~

Cadaver? I'm a person. What in God's name are you talking about? Kathryn you are taking my hospital gown off? Don't you dare!

Pat strained to move away. She had one toe that seemed to be working a bit. She can't seem to get leverage. Consequently she was lying there without any control of her body.

Leave my hospital gown on, please? Don't leave me naked. Oh my God, no you don't! I heard that, who has undressed me? Kathryn, I am not a piece of meat! I'm not a cadaver! Why am I undressed? Where am I? I don't recognize that male voice. Some man! Who in the world are you? Let's not use detergent either. That would be awful.

Kathryn. Who is that? Actually his voice sounds familiar now. But I can't place him. If I could I wouldn't want him touching my naked body. Help me out here!

Again, Pat tried to move her toe. It's cramped up. It won't move. It's not mobile.

Oh no!

~

Kathryn asked, "Can I help? Where do you want me to wash?"

Bernard smiled at Kathryn, "Sure, if you don't mind washing her private parts."

~

What? My private parts, you're going to wash me? Don't you dare! No, no, no you don't Kathryn! Nobody gets to do that but me. Get away from my breasts. Get away from my kootchie-coo. Why are you doing this? Kathryn, who is that? I heard that man. I'm on display aren't I?

She attempted again to move her toe.

Hrrr, Brrr, Pfft, Pfft.

I hope you don't use detergent. Now I know someone has to wash the body, but detergent... Isn't that a bit harsh? That will really irritate my skin.

~

Kathryn asked, Bernard, "Should I use disinfectant?"
"Yes by all means."

~

What? Help! Don't you dare, you're putting disinfectant on my kootchie? Oh my. I'm not a toilet. That will burn my private parts.

Are you all crazy? I'm not dead. I must be lying on a table naked. This is definitely not fair. Kathryn can't you see? I'm still alive. How can I get your attention?

Pat began praying, *Help me God, please. Just give me my charley horse back or some sign.*

~

Kathryn scrubbed her breasts front, top and sides, and back rear private parts with disinfectant. She then washed the front of her vaginal area. She said in a whisper, "Pat why are so darn hairy down there? Whew, done."

~

Kathryn, you're talking about my kootchie to some stranger! Well I don't get waxed like some people do. If that's what you mean. How could you? You're in big

trouble... I'll haunt you if I don't get outta here. Kathryn,
I thought you were on my side. HELP!
   Suddenly the charley horse came back.
Good. My foot's cramping.

~

Then she dried Pat off. There was a special cream that
she was recommended to use afterward. It's used in
funeral homes for cadavers. She carefully smoothed it all
over where she had washed. Since after one dies the skin
does not absorb moisture the cream is only used for
cadavers to smooth out their skin to have a slight glow.

~

Are you still washing me? Cover my body for God's
sake, Kathryn. Who was that man? Cover my breasts and
my kootchie-coo. Remember, I'm modest. I don't even let
Finnegan see me naked for goodness sake.

~

   "Good job," Bernard said with emphasis on it being
her first time. *"And* it was your first time. Great! I wish
you could help me with all the cadavers."
   "Thank you Bernard. I'll keep my day job though."

~

I'm being raped by some guy named Bernard. And Kathryn is being praised for washing my naked body. This is not right. I'm at the funeral home, not at a car wash. I'm naked. Holy cow!

Kathryn you better cover me... Please. Don't let him see me like this!

~

They wash the rest of her body with strong disinfectant. Kathryn carefully covers her private parts from her breasts down. But the towel is small and falls to the side.

Bernard is readying to insert eye caps. Kathryn snaps, "No! No eye caps Bernard."

"Okay. When will she be seen?"

"Not until tomorrow morning right before she's buried."

"They will prevent her eyes from opening."

Kathryn shook her head. "It's all about what Pat would have wanted. She emphatically stated, NO EYE CAPS. I saw her list of things and she capitalized that directive."

~

Eye caps... Oh my God! Don't put anything in my eyes Kathryn! Help! Help! I pray they don't use eye caps. Kathryn... If I ever get outta here, I'll be blind. That was on my list Kathryn. I wrote that in caps. Ask your husband. Ask Frank, Kathryn. He knows that was specifically on my list.

~

Kathryn did not put a face mask on and the smell of the disinfectant was getting to her. It was quite strong. She coughed for a moment of two.

Bernard asked if she needed a mask. Kathryn shook her head no.

~

I smell something mighty strong. It smells like Lysol. Wow! My smeller works. No wonder why you're coughing. What in the world? Why are you using Lysol on me?

Come on everybody. Look at me. My skin is too warm for a dead body. I must look somewhat alive. Well, this Bernard guy better treat me with kid gloves. Don't let him hurt me.

~

Bernard began washing her face with a strong scrub soap that's normally used in hospitals. Kathryn was amazed at the process. The washing was over and Pat was ready for makeup.

May came around the corner and could see her mother was naked. She asked, "Can we dress her first?" She covered her mother modestly with the towel that had fallen beside her. "I'll keep her covered Kathryn."

Kathryn was still busy drying the body. She nodded her head.

~

That's my girl. Cover me May! I knew my daughter would save me. May, watch what they do to me. Don't let them expose me or hurt me.

Speaking of pain, my finger hurts. I think I'll work on moving it. Pain is good. It shows I'm alive.

Pat attempted to reach the metal lip of the table. The lips are to collect fluids during a body washing. She pushed on her sore finger that can barely touch the table. She poked and probed and finally was able to make a slight sound.

Screech... *Listen up everyone.* Screech...

~

May with a surprised facial expression, looked around. "What was that?"

Kathryn looked at May and said, "Nothing. You're just nervous sweetie."

She brought out the one piece flannel pajama set designed with cute little pink poodles on them.

May said, "I thought I heard something come from that table."

Kathryn dressed her sister-in-law and said, "She sure doesn't feel dead. She has so much resilience and plasticity. I'll put her footie slippers on when her toenails dry."

May gaped at her mother with a questioning look. "Kathryn, you're right, she doesn't look dead. What if they made a mistake? Look at her. She just doesn't look dead to me."

~

That's because I'm not dead. Now for the past... I don't know how long of a time period, you've seen my naked body. Think about it. One of you, come on, you can do it. Tell them, 'Maybe she's not dead'. Touch my skin. Blood is still pumping. I must be warm.

I'm not dead! Now you've moved my arm, I can't reach the table.

You can do it. Just take my blood pressure. Or listen for a heartbeat. Some idiot doctor pronounced me dead. He should be fired.

I don't remember anything that happened in the hospital. I'm alive though, why didn't someone see that?

~

"She looks like she's just sleeping," May said quietly.

Kathryn said trying to ease her pain, "Yes, she really does May." May and Kathryn both began sobbing.

~

Bravo! That's the point. Now, let someone know, Kathryn. You are a registered nurse, aren't you? Both of you have to acknowledge that something isn't quite right here!

Now May, no crying. Just save me. This is not the time to lose it. Pull those boot straps up and ask the big questions to the right people. Tell Uncle Frank. 'She doesn't look dead. Why don't we check her pulse?' Use your gut instinct.

Kathryn help May out. You're the one who should be questioning this whole thing.

~

May looked at Kathryn, "Do you think maybe they made a mistake? Maybe she's not really dead? Look at her."

~

What did I say? That's right May. Maybe they made a mistake is right. That's my girl. Well answer her Kathryn.

~

Kathryn smiled and said, "Listen May, you're mother is definitely deceased."

~

No I am not!

~

"Now... What color do you think your mother would like on her nails?"
"The same color as her lipstick I guess?" May looked away. "Sure, sure. Pink I think."

~

Now May, you know I don't like pink... Unless it has some red in it. Now pay attention girl. I'm not dead and I don't want to look like I'm sixteen either.

~

Kathryn holds up a bright pink color. May shakes her head. "She actually likes a pinkish red."

~

Now that's correct. Hot pink is for teenagers. So don't use fuchsia. What are you two doing? May, I need you to help me. Forget the lipstick. I no longer care about how I look. Just check if I have a pulse or something. Please do the right thing. Save me!

She pushed on her finger again.

I don't know if I can do this right now.

She made a muffled sound with her finger. She was still on the metal table. The sound was drowned out by the conversation.

~

Kathryn handed May a pinkish red color. May carefully pressed the lipstick on Pat's top lip. "There I did it... Done!"

Kathryn said, "What about the bottom lip?"

May said, "Oh sorry, she gently pressed the tube on the bottom lip and the mouth felt too pliable for what she was expecting.

"Sorry Mom, that's all I can do for you. This bothers me too much. You felt too much like you were alive. Am I the only one that feels that way?"

~

May, May, what are you doing? You're losing it. That's all you can do for me? You were on a roll. You hit the nail on the head. I am alive! Keep that thought. I think I'm crying, maybe you'll see real tears. As hard as I try I can't seem to make tears.

~

May said, "Oh sorry Kathryn, that's all I can do. Can I hand you anything or do anything else for you? That's the best I can do for my mother, Kathryn. Why does she still feel soft, and pliable?"

"That will change. It's still early. I know how you feel. We're just about done. I'm going to polish your mother's finger nails and then I'm finished. She has flawless skin. I hope my skin stays as clear as hers when I reach her age."

~

Yes I do have perfect skin, because I stay out of the sun. But, I'm not dead! How am I going to get that across to you? I'm in a pickle here.

You two are dressing me for my funeral, aren't you? Oh, just great! How can I get your attention now? Let me try and wrangle enough moxie, or oomph to wake out of this crazy blank space in time. So this is what a stroke feels like. I do feel confused, but I don't feel totally helpless.

My toe hurts. Oh my, oh my. My foot hurts! I have a charley horse! It's back... Oh my... Keep going charley! You can hurt all you want. Look at my foot girls. Look at... I don't know which one it is. But I feel it. Look at it! May, you know how Mom gets those god-awful cramps in my feet? Just look at my foot. I don't know which one it is. But it's a mess. Look May!

~

Kathryn looked down at Pat's left foot. She noticed her toes were separating from each other. She immediately attempted to hide that foot from May. She thought that might be a reaction to chemical changes. She put Pat's slippers on her feet.

She said quietly, "They must be dry by now. There... There dear girl. Now your foot will relax."

~

Wait... Relax? What do you mean relax? Why is my charley horse gone? What did you do Kathryn? Okay, okay, I get it. You think if you cover the foot that it will relax. Well... That's because I am not dead! Let May see my foot. She'll know. You're a registered nurse, why don't you see I'm not dead?

~

Bernard walked into the room. "Do you girls need anything? Anything at all?" Both of the girls shook their heads. "Okay then," He said, "Are you okay Mrs. Burns?"

May said, "Yes I believe so. My mom looks good now, she is ready to go I think, and her hair and makeup looks perfect. She's already been dressed in her pajama attire. I tried to get her eternity ring off but I changed my mind. I want that to stay on her finger for eternity, anyway."

Bernard said, "We will put her in the showroom for the family to view for the next few hours."

Frank and Bo came into the room. Bernard and Bo lifted Pat from the stainless steel work table and into the casket. They all then assisted in carrying Pat into the showroom. Flowers were already streaming in around where Pat will be viewed. Now that Pat is in the casket, Frank fooled around with the bell and the tube that Pat had requested at her birthday celebration. The bell had fallen off the bracket a couple of times already.

~

I heard the bell Frank. But it keeps falling off the bracket. You better fix it. It might help save my life.

Pat attempted to probe around with her sore finger. She pushed and pushed but could not find the bell.

You'd better fix it before they even think about putting me in the ground. Oh my God! Don't put me in the ground, with or without that bell.

Frank, my dear brother, help me now. Please get me out of this predicament. If I get a hold of that bell, it'll be ringing like no tomorrow.

~

Frank worked on fixing the bell while Bo stood there gawping at his aunt. He'd grown a special bond with her.

"Aunt Pat... I'm so sorry you didn't get to go to the islands like you wanted. I could use a trip to the islands myself. I miss you so much."

Bo blew his nose and remained misty eyed while being vigilant. His mother Kathryn handed him a tissue.

"Mom, why does she look like she could just get up and go?"

"Because May and I were very particular of how we wanted her to look. I guess we did a good job."

~

Because all I need is a hot bowl of oatmeal. I'm perfectly fine.

Bo... My boy... I love you so much! I'm going to the islands someday. You'll see. We can both go. Don't you worry my boy? Please don't think I'm dead. They are wrong. You can see I am not dead. Look at me. I'm alive.

Talk to me son. I can hear you. Please talk to me. Say anything. I'll always love you.

~

Bo turned around and said to his father, "I can't look at her anymore. She looks like she could just get up and go out for a bite to eat. She looks beautiful."

Frank said, "Well your mom and May did a good job, if she looks that good."

~

Pat was feeling a bit weak now but wanted to work hard at getting someone's attention. She intently listened to Bo.

Don't cry my boy. I'm still here.

She was getting light headed. She continued to listen to the banter that was going on at her funeral preparation.

I think I'm falling asleep. Wake up Pat, you can't fall asleep. But I can't stay awake either. Maybe I am really dying. Don't think those thoughts. Stay alert, stay awake Pat.

Pat began to doze and soon fell asleep.

April 13, 1:30 p.m.

Pat awoke feeling more alive than ever. She wondered what exactly was supposed to happen in the casket. She couldn't hear anyone. They'd left her alone. She believed she was in that funeral home. The flowery scent was strong. But that just meant she probably only had twenty-four hours before they put her in the ground. Would she just die? She thought about that fun birthday celebration and how sweet, but sneaky, her daughter was preparing it. She remembered the list she gave her brother Frank and that he would probably be able to rescue her. Pat tried to think back to how the party depicted her death. Would they do it right?

She thought of seeing her pretty daughter again. Her appreciation of her granddaughter and her adorable smile... Oh how she longed to see her again!

She thought of May and how clever and loving she was. Her birthday party was a fond memory...

October 24, last year

May Burns was a thirty-eight year old sandy blonde with pretty, memorable hazel eyes just like her mother's. May and Pat both shared the same perfectly smooth as silk, flawless skin. May had her mother's beautiful smile. The two had been extremely close for many years.

May was a female image of her cousin Bo. Her seventeen year old daughter, Michelle, favored her Father Dan's looks with a fair complexion and big blue eyes.

May had been planning a special surprise birthday event for Pat's sixty-fifth birthday coming up. This was the big day Pat would turn into a senior with grace. Pat told May so many times that she would never reach the age of sixty-five. She said that ad nauseam. She would say 'That's how old my mother was when she died. And everything is starting to hurt and I sure don't want to get those big varicose veins like Mother'. May knew her mother had it in her to be proud to have reached sixty-five with few side effects. *A party will soften the blow,* May thought.

May and her Uncle Frank were very involved in the planning phase of the theme of the party. Pat was sure her daughter was up to something. May believed her mom needed to relax and try to reach sixty-five without looking like a deer in headlights. She needed to not worry so much. She needed to reach the point of not having to be perfect. She needed to hold her head high. Maybe her new relationship with Mark would give her a new outlook on aging.

The party would be at May's ranch house just a few miles away from Pat's. Hopefully it would bring Pat's sense of humor back. It was all about having a good time.

Pat had a sixth sense when something was up. Little telltale signs like *why don't you get your hair done Friday, and wear a certain dress.*

Pat said adamantly, "You better not do anything big for my birthday, Miss May! It's just another day you know."

"Mom, I want to take you out to a great restaurant with Michelle and Dan, and that's all. I just want to celebrate your life.

"Just make sure you don't plan anything else, okay? It's on Friday of course. Can you be ready by five?"

"Well, I guess so. Now you know that's not necessary. Okay, anyway plans, Hmm... Let me look at my calendar and see if I can fit you in."

They both laugh. Pat reached over and kissed her daughter, they both said "love you" in unison. May had turned toward the door.

The door bell rang just as May reached for the knob. Finnegan ran in circles frantically whining and wagging his whole body. May opened the door. "Hello Mark."

"Hello, how are you May?" Finnegan continued his total body wag. It was clear that Finnegan was crazy about him. Mark reached down and gave Finney an expected belly rub, since the dog had quickly rolled over reaching up with all four paws in anticipation.

"Well, see you," May said quietly before she left. She examined him as she hurried past. She whispered, "Old spice, I believe."

Mark looked at May as she waved and left. He reacted, "Huh?"

May thought to herself *shelves for the laundry room my eyeball.*

Mark was probably the same age as Pat, but nobody really knew. His thick head of silver hair was always perfectly styled. His attire was unique and sometimes flamboyant with bright colors, especially red. Even when the weather dropped below freezing the man wore shorts, showing off his good looking, tan, and muscular hairy legs.

May sprinted down the side walk to her car and glanced back looking at the door. "Hmmm!"

She was a half hour late for picking up Uncle Frank at the funeral home. He had some big plans ahead and had said, "Meet me at one p.m. pronto!" They had been planning this fun birthday party with a twist for a long time. She has to get all her ducks in a row now.

Suddenly May looked frantic. She searched in her pockets and emptied her purse on the sidewalk. "Where in the hell are my keys?" She searched all her pockets. "Oh damn!"

After a short greeting with a smile, Pat said, "Hi Mark. Thank God you're here. I need some advice. My daughter is planning on taking me out Friday on my birthday. I don't think I can handle it. She wants me to kind of tag along. They go to that fancy-dancy place, The South Side Steak House, with my son-in-law Dan. All he does is argue about the prices. It doesn't sound like fun to me. I'm glad they are bringing Michelle, my granddaughter, so I won't be bored. But I'm a token thought, I believe... Or maybe not. I don't know. What do you think?"

"Birthday? You never told me you had a birthday coming up. I would have asked you to the Toodle House. They have a rib eye special this Friday, and an all you can eat salad bar."

"Awww, I would have loved that."

"Pat, before I forget what I wanted to say about the shelves, let's go in the laundry room for a minute. I want to show you where we both made a mistake on that third shelf."

They both walked into the laundry room. He pointed to where the cabinet was just a hair to close to the wall to open. "You'll be banging your hand every time you open the cabinet. So let's just put two up there." He pointed at his observation.

"Oh, you're right. I'll have a broken finger before you know it. That will be absolutely perfect! You're a genius."

Just then the front door flew open and May bolted back into the house. She was clearly in a hurry. She zipped over to the kitchen counter. She then fetched her keys exactly where she had left them.

Curiously, Pat and Mark walked back into the kitchen. Pat goggled at her daughter shaking her head in disbelief. She laughed. "This happens all the time! Look at her... She would forget her head if it wasn't attached."

"May, Mark just invited me to dinner on Friday, also. Why don't we invite Mark, to go with us on my birthday? That would make sense. Don't you think?"

May spun around toward them. They were both staring at her. She said under her breadth, "Maybe 'Brut'... Hmmm... I wonder. That would work," May giggled. "There you go again Mom," She whispered softly, "And to think you might have been lonely on your birthday. You're a real mystery Pat Faros."

"Well now... Ummm... Sure," she stammered. "Why don't you meet us here at six?" she said, addressing Mark. "Just give me your phone number."

Mark nodded his head slowly, reluctantly accepting her offer. He reached in his pocket and handed May his card.

May noticed Finnegan was sitting on Mark's foot licking his hairy leg.

Pat looked perplexed. She said, "I thought the invitation was for five o clock".

"Oh yeah right, I'll talk to you later about that Mom. I gotta go!" She looked at her watch, "it's late, shit!" She high tailed out of the door.

Mark looked at Pat. "I can't really afford that extravagant sort of place. I'm just a simple man."

"Well, if you finish the job today I'll slip in a little bonus for the simple man."

They both snickered. Mark blushed as he was led by the arm back to the laundry room. Finnegan followed behind with his wiggly-waggly tail going full speed.

May walked out on the driveway and noticed Mark had parked his truck so that she could easily get out. It was parked behind her car at an angle. She thought, *Wow you're considerate too*. She stuck an invitation under his windshield wiper. Her thoughts were curious about Mark and her mother. *Finnegan even likes you. Go figure*.

An hour later Mark jumped into his truck and was surprised to see something on his windshield. He looked at it. It was a silly looking invitation. It was covered with photos of the Walking Dead style zombies. There was a picture of Dracula on the front with ghouls and ghosts together.

It read: You're invited. Remember, Pat doesn't know anything about it. So try not to let it slip. Come at your own risk. Beware of the living-dead. Wear your favorite zombie costume if you'd like or bring a covered dish or both, but just join us. We're celebrating Pat Faros' sixty-fifth birthday, at 5:30 p.m., October 25. Anyone dead or alive will enjoy the feast.

Where: May Burns house, 99 Largo Dr., Krum, Pa.

Phone: 645-5511.

He laughed and drove away.

October 25, day of the party

"**W**eird, I'd say!" Dan, May's husband, said, "This is really weird."

May's house was becoming Dracula's cave. It was full of webs, bats and spiders. It looked very much like a dungeon. May, Michelle, and Michelle's boyfriend Larry were decorating three rooms: living room, dining room and kitchen.

"It must be working if it's irritating your father" May said with humor in her voice.

Just for fun, situated at the back of May's living room was a brand new red cherry wood casket. It was built by her Uncle Frank who is a casket maker by trade. He had added an air tube and a bell attached to the lid, as Pat always said she wanted like some folks did in the nineteenth century, just to be on the safe side.

This one was absolutely beautiful! The satin lined inside was white with the initials PF in red, surrounded by red roses on the pillow. The outside was exquisitely hand carved with embossed red roses. The casket had a hilarious looking blowup doll representing the corpse. Someone was installing an eerie purple light attached to the casket for effect. Frank was orchestrating the design and held his thumb up to a friend of his who did electrical work for him.

"It looked great, Bill!"

Michelle was putting much emphasis on walking dead decor. Her boyfriend, Larry Booth, was already in his attire and brought over a bag of plastic spiders and fake blood. It looked like he had blood on his mouth and hands.

Dan said, "You're all a bunch of nuts." Even the napkins on the table looked like blood was on them. He said, "You're not getting me in one of those mummy costumes."

Michelle looked at her father with a grin, "Zombie, not mummy, Dad, There's a difference. Zombies are smart."

Larry said, "Mummies are just empty shells."

Dan looked bewildered. "I'm going to be a priest so I can get rid of all the undead around here... And the vampires. Or are they the same?"

Michelle shook her head and said to her father. "You don't know anything about vampires." Larry laughed in a low scary tone.

Dan just shook his head. "You two are really weird."

He changed into his cassock. His plan was to be a priest to fight off Dracula or whoever looked evil.

He was given the hefty task of creating two special punch drinks. Getting his bar filled with liquor and trying to invent a punch that would dilute the alcohol and have a tasty flavor was quite the challenge.

Mark stopped by early after talking to May. He inquired about helping out with some of the many fun details. He chose not to dress in a costume. He arrived dressed in black; but that was Mark.

Dan was working on food coloring the zombie drinks. Mark was in charge of the dry ice for the green punch, Zombie Juice, he was trying to make. It was turning out perfect.

Michelle and Larry had just finished with the last of the decorations. The rooms were very ghoulish. Streamers were everywhere with cottony webs and plastic spiders were situated on the furniture and hanging from all the doorways. A few gifts were wrapped in black shiny paper. One gift was wrapped in red paper with a black bow. Michelle turned on her music; it was from Phantom of the Opera. Larry was lurching around practicing his ability to walk imitating a real vampire.

Here at May Burns house the word hectic was a noun and running rampant in her living room and kitchen. May, happy with the food and decor, scatted away to get her shower and pick up her mother by five thirty or Mom would be suspicious. She would leave without Dan with an excuse for her mother simply being *he wasn't ready yet*. She'd have a lot of excusing to do. It was difficult at best in convincing her mother who was always suspicious anyway. May knew how her mother would react. But she was happily up for the challenge.

Michelle went into her bedroom to get into the undead costume of her Dracula attire. She was more excited than anyone. She said with her best Dracula voice, "I can't vate to see my Nan. Ve vill surprise her to death." As Michelle debuted Count Dracula, Larry and Dan said she was a 'dead ringer'.

Michelle or Dracula could be seen putting a last few spiders in candy dishes and covering a doorway with a web that had previously fallen to the floor. May grabbed her car keys from the kitchen counter and skedaddled out the door. She said with a loud announcing type voice, "Be ready for her. We'll be back in thirty minutes."

Straight away the door bell rang. It was getting late and people were arriving. When May arrived with her mother it would be a memorable surprise. Dan had already answered the door for the first zombie. The ghouls and living-dead creatures were already creeping into the house.

Dan designated Mark to take the covered dishes to the kitchen. Michelle was finding black paper plates and stacking them decoratively. She was gabbing with folks that she had already recognized. "Hi Vanda," she said. "Vee are so glad you could make eet."

Mark took Wanda's covered dishes and laughed at her hippy disguise. "Your disguise is cool man!"

Pat was in May's car asking, "Where is Mark? Where are Dan and Michelle?"

"I left them at my house. Michelle wanted to bring Larry and there wasn't going to be any room. And you know Michelle. She takes forever to get ready anyway."

That made sense to Pat. *Why was Larry going? Too many people*, she thought. *Why was May putting Finnegan in the car*. "What's going on May?"

"Well it's a nice evening and Finnegan likes to play in my yard."

That made sense she thought. "Wait May! I have to pee."

"We'll be at my house in a minute or two Mom. Can it wait?"

"Well, I guess I'll have to wait. Just hurry!"

When they pulled up May ran in first before her mother and she stuck her head inside the door and peeked at the ghoulie guests. "Are you ready for her?"

Michelle sitting next to Larry at the door, responded, "Yes vee are quite ready!" She whispered to the folks sitting near the door.

Finnegan came running up to the door barking. Pat was right behind him, she just plowed past May. "Where is everybody?" she asked. She suddenly came to a stop, a balloon popped. Pat jumped quite startled.

"Surprise! Happy Birthday Pat!" A group of people, some in scary costumes, jumped out. They came from the crowded living room and kitchen. A couple friends didn't have disguises. A group of ghouls and goblins were standing around in their scary and funny costumes.

A zombie startled her and she actually stepped back. "Oh my goodness, I just have to find the bathroom." She ran full tilt to the bathroom to prevent the unthinkable.

Finnegan began yapping and running around like a younger dog.

Michelle was in her Dracula disguise. Larry started swinging his cape around, looking pretty scary, smiling with his bloody looking fangs.

Pat came walking into the living room where most of the folks were congregating. She full on belly laughed at her friends making ridiculous fools out of themselves.

She shook her head. "You guys really outdid yourselves." She walked around the room looking at each guest and chatting with them, thanking them for coming and making it such a crazy but wonderful surprise.

Michelle responded "Yesss...Vee ver so anxious to see you." She was not recognizable. "Kiss me Nan!" she said while sticking out her lips.

Her boyfriend walked over to her and snuck a kiss. Pat jerked back. "What? Two vampires kissed."

Michelle moved closer to Pat and tried kissing her but Pat snuck away. "No thank you," she laughed. "That's way too weird. No thank you, not with all that weird scary makeup on."

May and Michelle and Larry couldn't stop laughing. Frank was walking around with his camera taking pictures of Pat and her reactions. It was good to see Pat laughing so hard.

"I haven't eaten all day. Do we have food?"

Mark walked over to her and handed her a roll up that looked like an eye. She immediately took a bite. "Delicious," she said, "Thanks. Where's your costume?"

"I didn't dress-up to scare you my dear. I dressed to please you."

Pat stared at Mark dressed in a sexy black long sleeve shirt with black slacks. He looked quite handsome and mysterious to Pat and that caused her to grin from ear to ear. They both laughed a good hearty laugh and walked around together looking at the different food choices.

She asked Mark if he knew all along. He laughed and nodded his head.

"They are, and you are, mean. No one told me," she said. "Well, I believe I'm going to need a drink tonight."

Finnegan came running following Mark and Pat who were heading over to the kitchen table full of wonderful hors d'oeuvres. Mark said with excitement, "Try one of those minis, pizzas, Rueben's, or two types of eyeballs. The rollups are good but those cheese eyeballs are the best."

She began filling her plate with eyeballs, Rueben's and two servings of mini pizza pies.

"I just had to go to the bathroom. At first I didn't see anybody? Finnegan was with me... *Why are you here*, I thought? I think I pushed May forward as I plowed through the room, I hope I didn't hurt her. Then I came to a sudden stop when I saw that the room was full of... zombies. A balloon popped and I jumped. I almost had an accident. They got me good. Those goof balls! My heart was beating a mile a minute.

"Then a group of people in scary costumes jumped out. A few more were in regular street clothes, like Carol Rose, oh, and of course you. Sitting or standing and clapping their hands. I was glad I was able to recognize you."

Mark gave her a quick kiss on her cheek. "Happy birthday."

Pat blushed and looked around at all her friends and family. She looked at May and mouthed 'Thank you'.

Finnegan began yapping and running around wildly.

"Michelle took the cake. She was disguised in her vampire makeup... She kissed me on the cheek. I told her she couldn't. She ignored me. She was speaking gibberish vampire talk, I think. Anyway, I think she brushed up against me and now I have makeup on my cheek. This whole thing was quite a surprise. It floored me in a good way. I won't forget it any time soon."

Mark got a kick out of her story and had a hearty laugh. "You were definitely surprised!"

Larry, Michelle's friend, was walking around trying to scare all the women.

The casket had a blow up doll lying in it that had blonde hair. The bell was hanging near the head of the doll, in the front of the casket. The oddest sight is an apparatus with a longish tube attached to the lid and also the dolls mouth. An eerie purple light was coming from underneath the doll. Smoke was all around the casket. It looked like you were about to see Bella Lugosi at any moment.

"How very cool," she said.

They both grabbed a napkin to wipe their faces. There was red on them that looked like blood. Luckily, it didn't rub off. "Not very appetizing," Pat said, "But funny." She looked over at May, "This was truly fantastic, but have you all lost your minds?"

May laughed and said "Uncle Frank was responsible for most of it. He brought over all the decorations. He paid for it. We just put it together. Michelle wanted to make you laugh also she wanted to really scare you."

Pat smiled. "It worked, I'm delighted. Wait till I get him... Frank that is."

May said, "Dan wouldn't get into one of those mummy costumes. He wanted to be a priest. We need more priests to fight off all the vampires."

Michelle sprang out of nowhere, scary as all get out. "I veel put some better moozic on for zee blood fest. No vun ees safe tonight." She found different scary music that filled the air.

Larry continued walking around the room attempting to scare those in their street clothes. He said, "No one is safe here."

Michelle laughed. "Especially my Nan!"

Mark said the bewitching hour is approaching. It was time for a drink. Dan, dressed as a priest, was taking charge of the booze; after all, how often does one get to see a bunch of seniors acting ridiculous? Larry attempted to sneak a drink. Dan shook his head no and gave him a Virgin Death Wish.

Dan looked oddly appropriate as a priest in his cassock, serving smoking zombie drinks next to the casket.

Mark walked over to Dan and ordered a drink, shaking his head. "I don't know how to place an order."

Pat walked up next to him. She said, "I think you'd like Zombie Juice." She giggled.

"We only serve Death Wish or Zombie Juice, so I will be glad to assist you..."

Mark laughed, How about Zombie Juice? Dan handed Mark a green colored drink that was smoking. "Thank you father," he said with appreciation.

Pat shook her head. "Wow! What have I ever done to deserve all this?" She laughed. "I'll have a short Death Wish. Thank you Father Dan."

He said, "Maybe I can help you handle those demons."

Dan poured her a purple drink and whispered, "Bless you."

Pat reached for the drink and couldn't stop giggling. "You're good!"

Laughter and music filled the room. Mark and Pat walked over toward the casket with their drinks.

Frank joined Pat and Mark at the casket and described the details to them. He said, "The wood is cherry, a very hard wood. It should last for as long as you need it."

Frank and Pat had a good belly laugh. Mark looked a bit shocked. This was making him feel strange, watching his friend get so excited about a casket.

"And I'll see that you're not embalmed in case, for some strange reason, they pronounce you dead and you're still kickin', like you mentioned. In that case, you'll breathe through this tube that is attached to the lid. Also, for fun, I added a copper bell that will hang near where your hand will be resting."

Michelle walked like the living-dead over to the casket with Larry. Pat and Mark bug eye looked at the two vampires as if they were frightened.

"Nan, you haaave to open my present and you vill understand." Michelle handed a black shiny wrapped present over to her grandmother.

"Michelle, how are you going to get that horrible makeup off?"

"Vhat makeup?"

Laughter could be heard everywhere.

Pat opened the present to see her gift, "That's exactly what I've been looking for, and you found them. Thanks sweetie!"

"Nan, they're only simple white flannel pajamas," Michelle giggled, "At least they're flannel; I know you wanted flannel! I like satin myself."

Michelle showed everyone the little pink poodles on them. She handed a silly whistle from Larry to Pat. It was a red child's toy, but Pat took it and said, "That will be included in my casket Larry. You never know. It may come in handy. Thank you."

Larry tried scaring Pat and said, "You vill know when the time ees right. The vhistle vill let everyone know you are ready to leave you're coffin."

"How adorable." Pat smiled and bit into a hors d'oeuvre eye ball. "The cheese balls… I mean eye balls... Are divine!" She accidentally dropped it on the floor. Finnegan grabbed it and ran to the next room.

"Finnegan!" Mark looked over at Pat. He held his hand up implying he'd get the dog for her. She said adamantly, "He can't eat cheese."

She continued to open the gifts that were stacked around the base of the casket. A cute pair of pink and white footy slippers that match the pajamas were from Bo, her nephew, who was dressed as Frankenstein.

He was laughing at the prospect of planning a funeral in such detail. His date, Ellen, started laughing too. She was dressed as the Bride of Frankenstein.

A variety of other gifts like chocolate caramel candy and a bouquet of roses which arrived without a name attached to them.

Everyone started snickering. Pat looked over at Mark who was sitting at the bar talking with Dan and looked a bit embarrassed about the whole thing.

Pat said with a smirk on her face "What beautiful flowers! It says, 'Happy Birthday Pat!' No name on them... hmmm, I wonder."

Mark said, "They are pretty just like you." Pat smiled.

May rolled her eyes and headed toward the kitchen. She looked around and asked "Who made the eyeballs?"

Wanda waved. She was dressed more like a hippie, with a bandana wrapped around her head and with an eye patch. She spilled some food on her ripped, faded bellbottoms. "Damn!"

Sitting next to Wanda was Carol Rose who was dressed in a fancy green pantsuit; her hands folded on her lap. She was dressed in street attire. "This whole thing is kind of weird," she whispered as she handed Wanda her napkin. "That casket takes the cake!"

Carol looked at Wanda who was obviously having a great time. Wanda ignored Carol and said, "I made them... The eyeballs."

Someone hollered, "Those eyeballs are delicious."

Wanda jumped up and joined the gathering around the bar/food table. "Yum...I need the recipe for these brains. It's cauliflower, right? I have a few friends that could use them, brains that is."

May shook her head. "Just bake the cauliflower at 350 degrees for thirty minutes. Oh... And you have to baste it often with olive oil and... Umm... Tamari and cayenne pepper. Our family loves it. The pizza crust is cauliflower too, and you'd never know the difference."

"Wow," Pat squealed with excitement. "It's super! What a cake!" It was a chocolate devil's food cake with cream cheese icing ghosts covering the chocolate fudge icing. Two candles, a number six and five, were on top and Happy Birthday Pat was written crazily with red gel looking like blood. Dan lit the candles, everyone in the room sang Happy Birthday. Pat made a wish. She attempted to blow them out. But she didn't succeed. She giggled and tried again. "Pfft... Pfft... Oh come on! I can't blow out these two dawg gone candles. Let me try again. Pfft."

Wanda walked over and maneuvered her way next to Pat and with one *pfft* the candles were out. Wanda said jokingly, "I think your blower is off... My blower works."

"Yum... Your cake is delicious," Wanda conveyed with a mouthful and a bit of chocolate on her nose. She turned to Pat, "Delicious. This is one of the best birthday parties ever!"

Pat nodded and smiled. She looked like she was about to cry.

"By the way Pat, I want to talk to you about something that's been bugging me for a while... Oh, but this is not the time or the place."

Pat pretended not to hear her as she walked back to her brother who was inspecting the casket.

"That must have cost you a pretty penny." Pat quipped as she patted her brother on his back.

"You're worth every pretty penny Sis."

Pat held her chest and smiled at Frank. "Frank, I can't get over how great this turned out." They both looked at the details of the casket. They had an endearing brother and sister kiss.

Pat reached in her pocket book. "I want to give you something for all your work."

"I'll have none of it Sis."

Frank pulled a list out of his pocket that he had been keeping for Pat for many years; since she asked him to help May with all her funeral arrangements. "You may not have realized I've been taking notes. Me, Kathryn and May are in charge of making sure the procedures are up to par."

Pat looked at the list and started to cry. "I didn't know you cared that much to remember all the silly details concerning my funeral. Now I have an added component, a whistle from Michelle's boyfriend."

Frank looked at his sister with pride. "Thanks, I just hope you don't need it for many years to come."

A crowd of people began to leave.

Pat attempted to get everyone's attention. "Ahem! Excuse me everyone. Thank you all for coming. You're a blessing. You have outdone yourselves. I had a wonderful time. You are all the best. I love you all for doing this for me. As strange and eerie as it is, I love you guys for this. Thank you, thank you, and thank you. Drive home safe, please."

Someone turned on the overhead lights. The crowded living room and dining room full of friends and relatives dispersed into the night. All that was left were filled trash cans and lots of decorations to remove.

"Don't forget to take back those spiders Larry. Thanks for the whistle. We don't need the spiders but I may need the whistle. Thanks again." May laughed.

Next day, 8:00 a.m.

Pat stopped by her brother's house as a thank you surprise, early the next morning. She wanted to visit with him knowing he was an early riser like herself. She brought along a glorious box of warm cinnamon buns. This had become a tradition for both of them whenever the time called for it. They seemed to warm the soul.

As he opened the door somehow he knew what she was up to. "You didn't!" He said giving her a long tight hug.

"I sure did."

The house was quiet since Kathryn usually slept in on days she didn't have to work at the local busy hospital. Frank was usually up at the crack of dawn, if he wasn't working out he was designing a new custom casket.

Frank and Pat seated themselves at his kitchen table eating warm cinnamon buns and drinking strong brewed coffee.

"I was hoping that you would have stopped by to find out what you thought of the party, Sis."

She gave him a grateful look. She nodded her head and smiled. "It was a blast! The best party anyone could ask for. It was so creative."

Pat watched Frank butter his bun and she giggled a bit. He slathered butter all over the top of the bun, until the melted oozy butter seeped down deep into the already sticky gooey sweet roll. His sister laughed. "Whoa there Brother!"

"What?" Frank laughed too. "I know what tastes good, buttery and sweet."

"No question it tastes good, but all that fat going right into your arteries. Why not just have Kathryn bring home an IV from the hospital and inject it?"

Frank jokingly said, "But that wouldn't be any fun."

They both laughed.

Frank licked his fingers and then attempted to butter Pat's, but she raised her hand and said bluntly, "I'm good thanks. I love butter, it doesn't love me.

"Frank, you really outdid yourself yesterday."

"Well, May and Dan did most of the planning. I just tweaked it up a bit."

"It was marvelous. I mean it! You have helped me with everything all my life. I am blessed! The party was a great success. Everything you've done for me has turned out wonderful.

"Bo turned out great too. He's kind, polite, handsome… And so smart. The two of you have made me very proud of him.

"I don't want to cry this morning. Let's just enjoy this wonderful treat.

"By the way, I have Wanda's recipe for those eye balls. They were so delicious. Tell Kathryn I'll leave it on the counter, in case she's interested." Pat pulled the recipe out of her purse and laid it on the green ceramic tile counter top.

Pat attempted to convey enthusiasm in her voice, "Bo seemed to have a great time. Since his divorce he hasn't really had time to have fun. The girl friend, I think her name is Ellen... She's quiet but nice. She, I believe, was the Bride of Frankenstein. They both were terrific. Bo had me in stitches. I laughed so hard I dropped an eye ball when he walked around like Frankenstein. Finnegan found it. Mark tried to get it from Finnie, but it was too late."

"His sense of humor, he got from me, by the way," Frank teased as he opened another stick of butter.

Pat quipped, "And his love of butter." They both laughed.

"I want to show you something after we eat. I built my own casket. It is bea…u…ti…ful!" They both stepped outside and Frank opened the shed door and turned the light on.

"Wow! You really outdid yourself!"

It was sitting in Frank's workshop large as life.

"Are you going to store it there until you die?"

"No. Blain buys caskets from me. Sometimes I make specialty styles for him... You know, custom. Check out the wood. It's dark cherry wood just like yours." He pointed to the carvings, "You know I did that by hand." Pat said she loved it. "I'll keep it at Blains showroom. We'll make a mint on caskets just like this one."

"Okay then. So much for speaking about the comforts of death. Let's go back in the kitchen now since I didn't finish my bun. Let's finish the rest. They're to die for, literally."

Pat said that her casket was the best gift she ever received in her life. "My gift was so beautiful. I never imagined I would be so enamored by a casket. It's the best thing ever!" Pat made a silly face. "You went all out for me with all my wishes. You kept a list of the things I can't even remember. How did you remember everything?"

"Well, I listen and I know how you are. That kid Larry, Michelle's boyfriend, is kind of weird, but the whistle was genius. I put it in your casket." They both laughed.

Pat walked over to the sink and rinsed her hands that were covered with sticky syrup. As she sat back down to finish her coffee, she licked the syrup off her wrist that she seemed to have missed. "Um... So... So good!

"You are the best. I mean it. And I thank you. You actually spent hours of your time. It's hard to comprehend. Cherry wood with red roses on it couldn't be better. Now, make sure I'm buried in my pajamas... With socks. I don't want my feet to get cold. Then it will all be perfect. By the way, did you speak to Bo about the adoption?"

"No, not yet, it might take some time. Well, I wanted to but Kathryn wasn't ready yet. She said she felt Bo needed some time after his divorce. He has been a bit cranky, she said. He met a girl, Ellen, but I think he's still in love with Judy. However, he realized she's a lost cause. The fancy attorney she fell in love with I hear is running for congress. But Bo's got to get over her soon, or he'll be more of a wreck."

"Poor guy. Oh... Okay. Whenever you're both feeling ready will be just fine. There's no hurry. I'm just covering all bases. My life at sixty-five has crept up on me. I just want everything in place. But of course it's not all about me. Talking to Bo will not be easy for either of you. If I can help in any way, let me know. You two will just have to fix that guy."

"That's a tall order, but Kathryn and I will do it, Pat. Bo is coming over today; maybe today will be the day. Who knows?"

"You know I was just asking. You don't have to tell him until the two of you are ready," she said half heartedly.

Frank turned the oven on to warm the last couple of buns. "You know I think I want to be cremated and my ashes put in my casket."

"You worked so hard on your casket and you just want your ashes in there? That's odd. Have you told Kathryn? She'll need to know, since she's your wife."

"Yes I have it all written down in my living will. Remember Pat, everybody's different."

"I guess I should do that too. That way if anyone needs to make a guess, they just have to go over the list. Birthing a baby is difficult, but dying is complicated."

"Everything's covered, Sis."

"Okay, good.

"You know Frank, I don't want to change your mind, but if you die before me. We would want to *see* you first."

Frank looked intently into Pat's eyes. "You know you can have a viewing before you're cremated."

"I had no idea, what are you going to wear to your viewing?"

"What's the difference? Who really cares? I'll send you a copy of my decision. I may just wear a pull over and jeans and maybe tennis shoes. Or better yet, a leisure suit. See Pat, remember, not everyone likes the same things. That's what I want anyway."

Pat continued talking, "Well one thing is for sure about the human body, when you're dead you're dead and you *will* decay. Most of us know that. But there have been many mistakes. I don't want that to happen to me. You know like being buried alive."

Frank laughed. "Well if they make a mistake with me. No one will know, not even me. Ha ha."

"Oh they do make mistakes," Pat said, with a serious look on her face. "For instance: A ninety-one year old polish woman that was declared dead by a medical examiner, spent eleven hours in cold storage. Attendants noticed the bag was moving. When they opened the bag she was fine, so they sent her home. She said she was okay but she 'Had to warm up with some pancakes'. Can you imagine? Hopefully, when you're pronounced dead you really are and if they are wrong they don't embalm you. Then they can discover their mistake and revive you. I know I don't want to be put in a mortuary drawer. The temperature is way too cold. I want room temperature... And no freezer!" They both laughed. "I've been reading too much about that stuff."

Frank responded, "I know that premature burials occurred in the nineteenth century. That resulted in special coffins being designed; and some were even patented! Many coffins had a bell inside and an air tube just like I put in yours. It was attached to the lid that reached the mouth so the person could breathe. That kind of stuff doesn't happen anymore though. I just thought it would be fun for the party, but I'll make sure everything is in place. That is if you go before me."

Pat laughed. "Oh, just in case!" They both started laughing. "Now that we're talking about dying, let's finish up those yummy buns. What a way to go! Mmm... Aren't these delicious?" Pat grabbed another bun. "I planned on stopping with two, but I can't resist. I'm coming over more often. I'll make sure I bring these delicious cinnamon buns. They make you feel at home. They're so divine. I bought them at the Mart.

"Frank, by the way, I want you to make sure that May doesn't change the way I want to rest in peace. Look... Some doctors look and see: no heartbeat, no pulse, cold skin, blue lips, and they say 'Ah... She's gone. Wrap her up'. I've thought about this a lot. I don't want to die, but even more so, I don't want to be declared dead and stuck in the ground when I'm not!"

"You are so obsessed. They'll pronounce you dead or not. You got to have some trust in the medical community."

"I do, but they really do make mistakes."

Kathryn, Frank's wife, dressed in her bright pink robe, was standing in the hallway eavesdropping on the conversation. "Ahem!" She sauntered into the kitchen and opened the oven. She looked at Frank flabbergasted. Under her breadth she grumbled, "Just great!

"Ah…When were you going to tell me about your heart stopping breakfast?" She looked at Pat. "You know he's a diabetic. Oh… And look at all the butter you're putting on that, Frank. Good grief! Really! He's type one you know."

Frank rolled his eyes. "She makes sure I never have any fun."

Kathryn bent down, looked in the oven, and with a paper towel she grabbed a bun. She then took a big bite. She cried, "Ouch! Hot, but good.

"You know Pat, he's on insulin," she said as she chomped down on her bun. "And he shoots up all the time now. Right around the time he chooses to eat a bunch of sugar. He would just grab an insulin needle and poke himself in the stomach. Then he believes he's invincible, like he's good to go. He feels like he can eat anything. He just won't do without it. I gave up! I have talked to him until I've turned blue but it doesn't sink in. No wonder he went into the casket building business. He's soon going to need one!"

Frank shakes his head, "I work out every day. I also see the doctor twice a year. The last time I saw him he seemed pleased with my progress."

Kathryn smiled, "Oh, he see's you survived another year, that's your progress."

Pat looked confused. She put her bun down on her plate. She felt like she had just caused an undue rift. She was now worried about her brother. She looked at Kathryn who was a nurse and said, "I'm so sorry Kathryn." She then looked at Frank with a questioning expression.

"Frank... You're on insulin now? I had no idea!" Pat got up and walked over to the sink. She poured out a half a cup of her now cold coffee, wiped her face and said, "Okay then guys."

Kathryn stopped her and said, "Don't go Pat, it's like a broken record in this house. I have this conversation with your brother every day."

She looked into Kathryn's eyes. "But I don't."

Pat smiled and held onto the kitchen door, she said, "I'm expecting a handyman at my house in an hour anyway. Huh, insulin now? I had no idea. Anyway guys, thanks for everything."

Pat left. Looking at Frank she mouthed a silent *sorry*. She then said, "Bye, love you guys."

That afternoon

As Bo Brigham, a forty year old computer software engineer, walked through his parent's spacious living room, he noticed his fifth grade school picture was still on the mantel of the fireplace. His picture of his first holy communion was there as well. But his wedding picture was gone. He wondered why. He still had strong feelings for his ex-wife Judy. She was beautiful the day of their wedding. He found himself thinking about her and with a big sigh walked over to the kitchen and called for his parents who were expecting him.

"Mom, Dad!" There was no answer from either of them. He opened the proverbial refrigerator door, looking for something... Who knows what? He examined everything and grabbed a bottle of cold water.

He believed his parents were probably shopping. They always made a big deal when he was expected to stop by.

He sat down at his parent's tidy kitchen table staring at his two letters. He had a second letter in his hand that would finalize his new life that was about to begin. He looked the table over. He really never took a good look at it before. He grew up with many fond memories at this round, honey oak table that had been in their family for two generations. The combination of lemon and linseed oil created a mild comforting scent which was pleasantly familiar.

The matching credenza which faced the seat opposite him was topped with a large beveled mirror that was hanging next to a painting of his grandparents and their three children. It was a great family portrait. It was as good as a photo he thought. His Aunt Pat had painted it. She was a very talented artist. She framed it with a beautiful antique gold frame. The mirror beside it gave the room a more spacious appearance.

He rubbed the table with his forefinger noticing the grain of the wood was smooth and never lost its shine. The house felt warm and inviting and kept that same feeling thirty years later.

This letter that his Aunt Pat gave him was before his divorce. She knew he was having marital difficulties and asked him to wait and open it with his parents present. She told him that it had to do with himself, his parents and herself. But she asked him not to open it right away. She said it would be better when he was in a better frame of mind.

He'd been dragging his feet about the letter for some time now, but today was the day. His father asked him to bring over the letter. He'd dreaded a conversation about what was in the letter? It had left Bo perplexed. But he chose to never open it. He loved both of his parents and didn't want to cause any undue heartache for them. He did have a suspicion of what was in it.

His parent's kitchen was small but had recently been renovated to extend it to have part of the dining room become a small office. Most of the space from the dining room was where the table formed a kitchenette. Bo liked the new arrangement better. It felt like there was more room. He can hardly remember using the dining room for dinners; they were always on the small honey oak table anyway.

Bo was considered handsome. He had a perfectly chiseled face according to the women in his family. According to his mother his face was similar to Clint Eastwood. Also, his grandfather on Frank's side. He had the same chin with the same dimple. Even though this man may not be his grandfather his resemblance was enough to believe it anyway.

He had a strong religious upbringing which caused some mild upset to his family upon his divorce. He knew he had been adopted but he never inquired as to who or why. There was never a conversation about it. His childhood was a happy one. No regrets.

He had always wanted to have a child but his ex-wife was not interested. He understood and never pressed her about it. She was more interested in advancing her career. She was a fine attorney that was working for the state of New Jersey as a state judge. They moved close to her district, bought a beautiful new home, and she seemed to be happy. She worked many hours and said she loved her job. This caused her to have dinner with friends and late nights away from home. Subsequently, Bo found out her friends were all men. Especially one man in particular. So they split. He left and offered her the new house they recently purchased together. Bo moved back to Krum and rented an apartment near his family for the time being.

He believed he had been adopted at an early age, but never showed an interest in locating his birth parents. Someone wanted him to know. When he was a young teenager he found his birth certificate. He started to read it, and then he was caught snooping, so he only remembered his father's name. The father it said was George Faros. He didn't have a chance to see who his mother was. He put the birth certificate back and pretended he didn't see it.

Since he had a relatively happy life he never complained, and never wanted for anything growing up.

It was five years ago when he found out he was given a different letter, written to him by his dying Aunt Martha. The letter said he was always loved by his birth mother. She knew that he would have a perfectly happy life. Being an unwed mother and not being able to raise a baby would have possibly caused much misery to him and the family.

He wondered, was Aunt Martha his mother. He wasn't sure. It was very dramatic. But then Aunt Martha was sick for the past few years before her death. He now realized his Uncle George was definitely his natural father but wondered was his real mother Pat or Aunt Martha. To him it didn't matter.

The letter from Aunt Martha read:

Grandmom was a widower and when Grandpop died she developed a string of ailments pertaining to her heart, preventing her from holding a job very long. Consequently food was difficult to put on the table with money so tight. Your mother at the age of eighteen would not have had the ability to give you a very happy and wholesome life. You were kept in the family so as not to cause additional stress. When you're mother, Kathryn, had to have a hysterectomy after she was newly married to your dad, it was evident that she would never be able to bare children of her own. So, what would be in the best interest of everyone was adoption. If you want to know the complete story contact Frank, your dad. You were loved Bo.

So, knowing that his parents were already a part of his current family he was pretty sure he knew who his mother was, so he wanted to wait and speak to his dad, who was due to arrive momentarily.

The two of them, Pat and his dad, were all that was left of his dad's siblings. Aunt Martha was gone. Aunt Pat and Dad were super close. Maybe his mother was Aunt Pat, after all, she was married to George.

Bo had attended his Aunt Martha's funeral, and it was pretty obvious that she was a probable candidate for his mother also. Aunt Martha had left him a good portion of her estate. This was a very odd event he thought.

Also, Aunt Pat has been writing to him once a week all his life. He thoroughly enjoyed the letters but in the past he thought they were tedious and busy for living only an hour away.

He thought about his grandmother's funeral and how Pat treated him like a son holding his arm and asking him to drive her to the grave along with her daughter and granddaughter. Everything was a bit curious to him. The giveaway was whenever she hugged him. She held him so tight and repeatedly verbalized his formal name

Beaufort, which he hated, over and over, at least five times just prior to releasing him from her Velcro grip.

Bo began sobbing. He sure did appreciate all the love everyone was giving him. But he missed Judy and needed to speak with his parents about that.

If only he had spoken to his Aunt Martha one last time to tell her how much he appreciated her. "I can't get over it," he said aloud. "Aunt Pat or Aunt Martha, my mom. Hmmm..."

Bo, still sitting at his parent's kitchen table, stared at the letter that his Aunt Pat gave him. The subject was: I have cancer and may not live very long. I want to tell you something very important. I love you and always will. You've made your parents and me very happy. God Bless you my boy!

He speculated, *She did say,* 'my boy'. *Hmmm.*

The letter from Aunt Martha had given him the choice to ask who his parents were. But Aunt Pat had implored he wait to open her letter until after his divorce because she knew it had been pretty devastating and broke his heart.

The kitchen door suddenly snapped open and his mother and father walked in looking worried. They asked

if everything was okay. They found it a bit unusual to see
Bo just sitting alone at the table.

"Yep, I'm just fine Dad."

They both sat knowing that everything was not fine
and they kind of knew what has been on Bo's mind. Pat
told Frank this day would come.

Frank's eyes began tearing up and he pulled out his
wrinkled handkerchief as he began to unravel Bo's story.
"You know that I didn't want to tell you the truth because
I didn't want to start a family feud or any kind of sadness.
I didn't know how you'd take the truth. It's no secret now.
The letter will clear everything up."

"It doesn't matter who my birth father was. You two
are my parents, right? I guess I've known for a while who
it... Probably was. But I didn't say anything, so as not to
upset anybody. Am I right?"

Frank nodded his head.

Kathryn held her face and began to cry. "I'm so very
sorry Bo". He shrugged it off. He stood up walked over to
his mother and gave her a great bear hug.

"I love you Mom. You'll always be my mother.

"Look." Bo reached over to hold his mother Kathryn
who was sobbing. "You're my parents. You both raised
me. I will always love you. And that's that! I will always
think of you two as my parents. Okay?"

"Aren't you going to open the letter?"

He put it in his pocket. "Maybe I will some day."

Kathryn looked up at Bo and said, "You are the best son any mother could wish for."

Frank stood up and reached to shake Bo's hand. Bo grabbed him and gave him a hug rocking him back and forth.

"I love you Dad."

He began to open a letter. They both looked at him confused. "This is not *The Letter*. This is my divorce decree. I wanted to show the both of you. I am officially divorced. I gave her everything. But the problem I'm having is I'm still very much in love with her. So, bear with me. I don't know why but I love that woman. She was my everything. But now she's brought her new boyfriend into our house. He's living there with her. Imagine that? They are sleeping in the same bed and everything. It's not going to be easy for me right now. I still love her."

Kathryn said, "Well you can move back in here if you want."

"No thanks Mom. My apartment is two blocks from work and Sal's Hoagie Shop is in walking distance. That's a plus."

"Well then, that's settled." Frank looked at his son.

Bo wondered what he meant. "Settled?"

"Yeah settled. We bought you a hoagie from Sal's. Your favorite is a cheese steak hoagie. That's still your favorite, right?"

"Oh yes!" Bo's face lit up with the ear to ear smile that grabbed his parent's attention.

"That's settled then, we did the right thing."

Frank and Kathryn started unloading the two bags that they had set on the counter. They all half heartedly laughed.

"Let's eat!"

April 12, 9:30 a.m.

It was early morning, about half past nine, and a tad chilly for April. May had stopped over to visit with her mother Pat. They often had breakfast together. Finnegan began barking. She looked around and noticed her mother, who was usually sitting at her counter working a crossword puzzle and drinking a cup of strong black coffee, was not home. She looked in the garage and didn't see her car. She had to go through the laundry room where Finnegan was quarantined, since he was peeing on the hardwood floors.

She thought to herself *Good decision Mom* as she walked passed Finnegan. She bent over the gate to pet Finnegan since he was rarely alone.

"Hi squirt!" She laughed. "Did your mommy leave you alone?"

She saw a black magic marker and a notepad next to the washing machine. She left a note. I was here and had some coffee.

She walked over to the coffee cup caddy in the kitchen and snatched her favorite cup. They were all fruit cups. She always chose the apple cup. There was just enough coffee left in the pot for one more cup.

She then sat at Mom's stool and saw she had missed a word. She read out loud. "What's a three letter word that means a stupid person? 'Oaf'," she said aloud. She filled it in. "There."

She looked around the kitchen and then got up and went into her mother's office.

"Oh, that's right. You probably had an early hairdressing appointment today."

She looked at the calendar and said, "What? You're at an attorney's office? Now I remember Mom. You told me you were going to change the will. But I didn't think you meant right away."

She looked on her desk as if to find something that her mom didn't want her to see. Suddenly she felt a bit guilty for snooping.

Her mom's office was neat; everything had its place. Her desk was clean. There were no papers to root through like the top of her own desk. Nothing was obvious to spy on without snooping around.

Her will was supposed to be written in concrete. She thought Mom was going to leave her everything. But now that she suspected that Bo was her natural child he would get a large portion of the inheritance. *Oh well,* she thought. She really liked Bo and was sad to learn he was getting a divorce.

Bo was her only cousin at one time. Now she believed she had a brother who she loved.

She looked around one last time and saw a book sitting on top of a folder. *Hmmm.* She peeked and there it was. It was a hand written letter from Patricia Faros. It discussed her will. Bo would get half the house and half of her finances. Well that was pretty clear and she didn't want to upset the apple cart. So May quickly placed the letter back in the folder then she slipped it under the book.

May walked into her old bedroom that Pat gave to Michelle whenever she babysat for May. It still had the pink flowered bedspread that was still covered with all her old stuffed animals. An original Barbie Doll sat on the dresser and a hand knitted blanket with pink ponies on it draped her overstuffed chair that she always loved. It was all exactly as she remembered it. She sat down on the chair and thought, *Mommy thank you for giving me such a beautiful childhood.*

As May left she kissed the teddy bear that sat for many years on her old sweet bed that always gave her that special feeling of being loved.

The phone began ringing. May decided to pick it up. "Hello. Pat Faros residence."

On the other end there was a pause and then a hang up. She said out loud, "Whoever it was, they didn't want to speak with me. Oh well." She decided it was time to leave.

An hour after May left Pat arrived home with a special treat for Finnegan and a bottle of white wine. She walked through the laundry room and picked up Finnegan and hugged him. Finnegan was so very excited to see Pat that he had a slight accident while she's holding him.

"Wait buddy." She runs outside and puts him in the backyard on the grass. He pees for a long time. "Poor boy, I'm sorry! It's my fault."

Pat played with Finnegan for a while and watched him enjoying a toy that had a treat inside it. He loved it!

She noticed the note saying that May had stopped by and had a cup of coffee.

"So you were here were you? Why didn't you take Finney out to pee? I asked if you ever stop by and I'm not home to please let Finney do his wee wee.

"Finney, I love you. Would you like to go for a walk my poor boy?"

The phone began ringing. Finney got so excited Pat was afraid he would pee on the floor again, so she let the phone go to the answering machine. As she was walking out of the house she heard a familiar voice on the machine, Hi, it's me, Mark. I was wondering. If... Well I'll call later, Bye.

Pat thought with deep exhaustion, *Mark you are so special. I can't wait to see you. But today is not the best day. I feel kind of light headed and I'm definitely taking a nap after I walk Finnegan. I hope you can wait until tomorrow. I don't know what's wrong with me. I feel sort of dizzy now.*

"Let's go Finnegan, let's get this walk over with."

April 14, 10:30 a.m.

Pat thought about how proud she was of her nephew Bo. She knew what she did when she was a teenager and was pregnant. She and her mother decided to offer the baby to her sister-in-law who was not able to get pregnant. It was the right thing to do. No regrets, she was at peace. Her life was now complete.

Pat also remembered how she felt the day before her medical event. She thought she was having difficulty getting a deep breath. Maybe she should have called her doctor. Pat began working on some breathing exercises. She took small quick breaths and then one long full breath.

She was feeling a bit better than earlier.

I wish I could talk. Maybe I can work on that.

In her mind she talked but her mouth couldn't seem to form words. Her attempts to move her lips were for naught. But she worked on it like an exercise. She was frustrated and exhausted. She huffed and puffed but could not open her mouth no matter how hard she tried.

Pfft... Pfft... Hmmm... Hmmm... Pfft... Pfft... Whhho... Whhho... Pfft... Pfft.

Well I can breathe. Now I need some water.

Her mouth was drying out and she felt parched.

~

Mark walked into the funeral home to view Pat before anyone else arrived. He looked at her. "My God, you look beautiful. You're stunning!"

~

Is that you Mark? My sweet hero! Now look at me. I'm getting a bit lethargic. Don't I look alive? Right? That's because I am. Now save me this time. Don't desert me. No one gets it. I've missed you. I know you've missed me, now get me out of here! I want to feel your arms around me.

~

"I shouldn't have left you the other morning. I knew you didn't look quite right. You weren't making any sense. You looked pale. You talked with a bit of confusion. Maybe I could have made a difference if I just would have told someone. I thought about it. But I chose to not do anything about it. I'm so sorry. Now look what's happened. I think... No I know, I had fallen in love with you. Because of me now you're dead and I may have been the one person that could have saved your life. I'll never forgive myself."

~

Don't beat yourself up. You said you loved me. Awww... Look here, I know, I know. If you would have told someone, that possibly could have made a difference. You could have been a hero. That's history. But you can be a hero now.

You really love me? Well if you do, Just get May or Frank's attention and tell them. I'm not dead. That's why I look so good.

Touch my hand... Go ahead Mark. I won't bite. Why won't you touch me? You're afraid I might feel alive... That's because I am!

~

"I feel like I want to touch your hand. I needed a hug from you the other day but I just left. Just a hug. But that's not going to happen now. Maybe I could just touch your arm. But what if they see me? I'll be so embarrassed."

~

What a wimp! Touch me you fool!

Pat attempted to reach the bell. She tried but it seemed to require more energy then she had.

Humph! I tried. This is hard to do.

Pat's eyes seemed to be opening slightly.

Look at me Mark! What do you see? I can actually feel my blood pumping. Now touch my hand. I think I see light.

She pushed her arm, it wouldn't move. She tried with all of her strength to move her hand. Inhale, exhale, inhale, exhale.

~

"Oh my goodness Pat, your eyes! I think you opened them a bit."

Mark touched Pat's folded hands that are holding a white lily. He turned around to see if anyone was looking. When he looked back at Pat he noticed one hand was to her side and the other had squeezed the lily. But the biggest concern was she felt like she was alive. She wasn't cold. He expected to feel stiff hands.

"How did your hand move to your side? I didn't do anything."

Frank walked into the viewing area and shook Marks hand. "So sad isn't it?"

He blew his nose. "She was talking about going to the islands in the near future. Maybe to the Bahamas or Cancun. So unfortunate, isn't it? I told her she should take a trip before it's too late. Imagine that. So sad."

Mark said, "Yes it is. I would have liked that myself." He noticed many family members were filtering in. He stepped back from the casket.

Frank said, "You don't have to leave."

"It's okay, I don't want to hog all the attention. Something doesn't look right though."

Mark wondered how Pat's arm had moved. *Maybe it just fell. Well that was weird.* He wondered how in the world that had happened.

Frank said, "Someone moved her arm to her side. I guess that's alright, but as long as she didn't move it. I moved her hands onto her stomach holding a lily. She looked like she was just sleeping, don't you think?"

"I don't know, kind of."

~

Come on Frank. How did my arm move? Think about it. Mark didn't move it. That's for sure. I moved it. Exactly what you're thinking. You are correct. Now don't

put it back. I'll just move it again. I can move my left arm.
I'll try and move the right arm, that'll clue you in. It's my
sore finger that helped me move my arm, I think.

Pat worked on that sore finger one more time. The
moment she realized she could slightly control that finger
she felt empowered.

It works! My finger is still alive!

~

"That's so weird. He looked at Mark. Did you move
her arm?" Mark shook his head.

He said, "No. I also wondered about her arm."

Kathryn came into the room and put a purple
hydrangea on the corner of her casket.

"There was a person I never heard of. The name on the
flower was signed Barbara Stetson and it said, 'I'm so
sorry'. It's so pretty your mom would have loved it. What
happened to her arm?"

Frank shrugged his shoulders.

Most of the flowers that surrounded the casket were
purple. Mark sat in a chair and watched every move the
family made. He said quietly, "Pat's favorite color was
purple, nice."

"Hi Wanda," Frank said.

"It's Nancy and Wanda. Good bye dear girl. We'll see you in the next life."

Wanda said, "I'll pray for you my good friend. You're probably blissfully in heaven. Maybe if I'm real good I'll see you there someday."

~

Wanda, don't go. I'm not dead girlfriend. Please help me. I'm not in heaven. They have me in a casket now and soon they will close the casket. Then I'll probably be in that dark temporary place.

Well I can't see anyway, but I think I can see light. So closing the casket won't really make much difference to me, but I'm afraid I won't be able to breathe.

You've got to help me, please. Where's that tube? Where is Frank? Now with my finger at my advantage Wanda might be able to save me.

~

Frank walked up to the casket and attempted to fix the air tube and bell. He also placed the silly red whistle near her hand. He smiled. "You might need it. I should have thought of that."

~

I feel the whistle and the air tube. We're getting there. Yuck, my mouth feels so dry. Now I'm so thirsty; could you give me something to drink?

~

The pall bearers closed the casket and walked it outside and down to the gravesite. They opened the casket one last time, per Frank's instructions. As soon as that happened rain drops sprinkled on everyone including Pat. Her face was getting quite wet.

It was a short rain shower out of nowhere. The rain droplets landed on Pat's cheeks and lips. Someone wanted to protect her from the rain shower so they closed the casket one more time.

~

What in the world? What just happened? I was getting a much needed drink. Frank you're probably responsible. Now open it up again please. I need just a tiny bit more water.

Pat tried to open her mouth. It wouldn't open but some rain that gathered on her lips had penetrated into her mouth.

Okay, that's a start. I needed that so much.

~

The rain was no more than a minute in time, and it was gone. They opened the casket one last time.

Carol walked up to the casket and said, "Well dear girl, here I am. I wouldn't miss this for the world. I'm sorry I didn't get to your house sooner.

"I think we're going to get a deluge. I don't mind getting a bit wet. But I don't want it to get you all wet.

"It might have made a difference, if I would have gotten to your house just a bit earlier.

"I love you Pat. You may not believe that. I only wish I could have done more.

"Wow, you sure look good! I love the color of your lipstick... And it matches your nails. Nice job.

"Someone should pat your face dry. It's wet from the rain shower."

Carol took a tissue from her purse and gently patted Pat's face. No one seemed to notice.

~

Wait, Carol, I was collecting droplets. Now what am I going to do?

*You love my lipstick? Well then, there is one favor Carol. If you set me free, if you save me, I will be your best friend and never doubt your word. I don't care what anybody says about you. And they **do** talk. I will defend you to the end.*

And you can have the lipstick and the nail polish as a bonus. Please just help me. I need a good drink of water.

Oh... And thanks for thinking about me. But don't blot my lips. That's how I'm getting a drink.

Oh good. It's starting to rain on me. That feels so good.

~

A teaming rain squall appeared out of nowhere. Carol ran under the canopy.

~

Pat's face was completely saturated.

This is great! I can feel the rain water in my mouth. Carol you brought me good luck. You're the best, thanks.

~

The minister John Boyd and Frank quickly closed the casket, concerned that the rain was getting too heavy and the inside of the casket would get too wet. The procession of family and visitors tried to gather under the outside canopy.

Frank announced, "Sorry, everyone we had to close the casket before the funeral. Pat would have wanted to be dry, warm and cozy."

The rain stopped as quickly as it started. They walked with the pall bearers about a hundred steps to the plot, hoping to avoid more of the downpour. It finally seemed to have stopped.

~

Wait... What's going on? I can't breathe as well. Where in God's name is that darn tube.

Pat worked her only moveable finger around the inside of the satiny covering.

I can't quite reach it. I know it's there. Let me try one more time.

Humph. There, it's touching my lip. I've got some rain droplets in my mouth. This is good. I've got this.

She took a deep breath.

Whew! That was scary. I sure did need that itsy bitsy amount of water. Now the tube is in my mouth. It's not easy inhaling. I guess, Pat, you're going to have to make do.

She took several deep breadths.
There you go girl.

~

Pat's funeral was at noon, very simple. Her son, her daughter and her husband, her granddaughter, her younger brother and several of her friends, including Carol Rose from the neighborhood as well as several other less familiar friends and acquaintances. Also there were several of Pat's friends from work and Larry, Michelle's boyfriend and of course, Finnegan the dog.

The funeral was outside on the grounds of the cemetery. The rain had finally stopped. This is what Pat wanted: simple, small, and outdoors.

Her brother Frank was officiating for the ceremony. A woman by the name of Diane Price walked over to Frank and gave him a hug. Frank was shocked she knew him because he had no idea who she was. She only said, "Your sister was the best."

It was quite beautiful. The temperature was warm with the sun shining. It was especially lovely. But the weather man was calling for more showers. They put the casket onto a casket trolley and the line of guests encircled the plot.

~

I can hear them. They are getting ready to bury me now. Oh no! I hear you Frank. Somebody please help me. Don't let them put me in the ground.

12:00 noon, funeral

"Good afternoon. I'm sorry this funeral was put together at such short notice but we can't control death. Sorry for the rain, but we can't control Mother Nature either. What was important was that I kept my sister's wishes in order.

"My name is Frank Townes Brigham, brother of Patricia Brigham Faros. She was youngest of three siblings. I would like to share with you some of my warm memories of my baby sister, Pat.

"She was a wonderful mother of May Burns, who she adored. When she became a grandmother of Michelle Burns, the world revolved around her. She had a special bedroom that had been May's and was now Michelle's.

"Me being her favorite and only brother, we spoke just about every day.

"By the way this must be good luck. I believe it's stopped raining.

"Any way... Patricia worked for over twenty years with the Johnsville High School and was one of the finest art teachers that they ever had. Dr. Ben Gey, can attest to that."

A snicker is heard and Frank blows his nose to drown out the giggles.

"All her students loved her and hated to hear that she retired five years ago."

Frank looked at Dr. Gey who shook his head and folded his hands.

"My sister, Pat, was the most generous and selfless person I ever knew in my life. I called her volunteering a gift that she considered her hobby.

"Together, I would like to acknowledge and share both our joy in the treasure that her life was to us and the pain that her passing brings to all of us. Pat was only six months past her sixty-fifth birthday when she passed away.

"She rescued Finnegan who was the apple of her eye.

"Finnegan, a sweet miniature French Poodle, was left for dead in an abusive, neglectful puppy mill when he was just a year old puppy. He needed surgery to survive.

She didn't blink an eye at the high cost of saving him. He was one lucky dog for my sister to adopt him.

"When she first saw him and heard of his tragic beginnings, he was hers. She didn't ask the cost and she stuck with him through his ordeal until he recovered. When she brought him home he was her baby. He was deaf but you'd never know it. A bit arthritic, but he's very well mannered. He has become a healthy beautiful dog and such a loyal pet!"

Frank was pointing at Finnegan whom Kathryn, his wife, was holding on her lap. Finnegan suddenly barks. Everyone quietly chuckles. He jumps down scratching at the dirt surrounding the casket.

"My sister influenced my life in so many ways. She graduated with a fine arts degree from Temple University. Her desire was to teach handicapped children art from their perspective. I cannot remember them all. But she had a few favorites that she took under her wing. One is here right now. His name is Sean Pitt and he has clients and creates personalized cards. I've purchased Christmas cards from him myself.

"She taught us to love with all our heart, always remembering to keep your family close, oh, and your dog. She loved her dog Finnegan.

"She volunteered at a local nursing home and brought along Finnegan who she had trained as a therapy dog.

"She taught oil painting and general art classes, which were a great success. Finnegan came along and was such a hit at the senior center that when she left him home one day it caused a ruckus. She had to promise he would be back the next class.

"Once, one of the students won first prize in oil painting at the local Krum Art Festival. That changed the man's life. He thanked her and cried tears of joy. At the age of eighty-eight! I'm tearing up just thinking about that day. Pat cried too.

"Our grandmom was sick, so Pat checked in on her daily. Then our mother was sick for a couple years and she checked in on her daily also. And lastly my youngest sister was sick for many years and Pat drove her to her chemo, her shopping and whatever she needed. She was always thinking of her family and others. She was their hero.

"Pat, you were my hero sweet sister. And I can't even begin to explain why."

Sniffling could be heard.

~

Frank, that was so nice. I was alive for my own eulogy. It was lovely.

I'm needing to breathe now. Now be a real hero and set me free. Get me out of here. I'm not dead everybody. No sniffles, no crying, no last words. Just save me now. You'll be my hero. Please help me. Come on Frank. Where's your concern when your sister is lying in her casket and **she's not dead?**

~

If anyone would like to speak, by all means please do. Finnegan barked. Giggling could be heard.

Suddenly Carol Rose walked up to the microphone that's propped up on a folding table.

Frank said one last thing, "Oh everyone, by the way, I want to thank Carol Rose for finding my sister and staying all day at the hospital with my niece, May Burns. Thank you Carol from the whole family."

Carol walked up to Frank and said, "Oh you're welcome, my pleasure.

"Hello family and friends of Pat Faros. I just want to say, my name is Carol Rose and have known Pat for many years. She lived directly across the street from me, and we became very close, once. She was such a wonderful person and couldn't do enough good in our community. I know she helped me so many times in my life. She helped me when my husband Charley died. She even officiated his eulogy at my church. To me she was the best."

~

Okay, okay Carol that's nice, I was the best. Now that's enough. Sorry to interrupt. We are no longer... Well you were good to May. You stayed with May throughout this ordeal? Wow, I'm surprised. I guess I forgive you. You are proving yourself.

Oh my, I think I'm getting dizzy again.

I think you actually were my closest friend once. Charley was a good man. George thought the world of him.

~

"Pat, I will miss you. And If I can do anything for your family, including taking Finnegan in, I would do it in a heartbeat. That's all I want to say." She glanced at May and Kathryn.

~

Carol, don't take my dog. Thank you for helping my daughter. Thank you for finding me, but not Finnegan.

Help me breathe!

May will keep him if I'm buried. She would never give him up. You hate my dog. Remember. You're too... I don't know if you could take care of a dog, let alone my dog. I'll not have it. May do not give Finnegan to that woman.

Somebody help it's hard to breathe!

Finnegan will be so unhappy. Oh no!

~

May and Kathryn smiled at her comment. They both silently thanked her.

A family friend and minister gave a blessing over the casket, "Merciful father, by your son's suffering and death and rising from the dead, we are freed from death and promised a share in your divine life. In the name of the Father the Son and Holy Spirit, one God forever and ever, amen."

May walked up to the casket with her daughter Michelle. They both kissed their finger tips and then touched the casket they both held each other and began to sob. May said quietly, "Mommy why did you have to go?"

Michelle said, "Nan, I can't believe you're gone. I'll miss you."

~

I can't see. But I hear crying. I'm at my own funeral. This is so strange.

May and Michelle stop your crying. I'm here, I'm alive. Now save me. I need your help. I'm not dead.

I'm a bit drowsy. Maybe I'll fall asleep. I don't want to fall too sound asleep. I need to wake up. I can't sleep now!

Where are you Finnegan?

Stop crying everyone. I'm the one who should be crying. I'll do all the crying for you.

I am not dead. This should not be a funeral. It should be a rescue mission. Help!

Pat's eyes rolled up into her head. She couldn't stay awake. The sun had been beating down on the casket so she felt quite warm and sleepy. A short bout of rain came down.

Let me get your attention if I can.

As tired as she was she was determined to get someone's attention.

This darn finger isn't working very well. Even my finger is tired. I don't want to fall asleep. It really hurts.

Hello everyone, I'm not dead! Let me try this finger again.

Ouch!

Scrrrtch.

~

A scratching sound could be heard. Carol turned her whole body around trying to get someone's attention. She looked at Frank. She mouthed, *did you hear that?*

"What did I hear?" Carol looked around. "Did anyone hear that?" She looked at Frank. He looked back at Carol wondering why she was talking right after the blessing. Carol was starting to annoy Frank.

"I hope we miss the downpour."

~

You heard right Carol. Frank, you should listen to Carol. She's beginning to make a lot of sense. At least once in her life, she's correct. She heard me. Let me try that again. Listen to this Carol!

She pushed her finger close to the bell and scraped as hard as her short nail could scratch.

Shhhhhhhtch...tch...Pfft.

Where's that darn bell? Where's that air tube? I've got the tube. But I can't quite get it to my mouth. So much for planning ahead Frank. I can't find either one now. Please put them where you said you were going to.

~

Carol eyeballed the casket for a moment. "There it is again. Did anyone else hear that? I heard something?"

She looked around at some of the folks that were standing near her in a questioning manner. No one else seemed to notice what she thought she heard.

She put her hand to her mouth. She said to herself, "Stop Carol! This is so embarrassing. Don't make a scene now. But... I know what I heard. I'm not crazy.

"Can I throw some rose petals on her casket before she is buried?" Carol pleads.

Frank nodded. There was a pile of rose petals sitting on a small folding table that was outside next to the casket. Just as Carol was about to scoop up a handful of rose petals Kathryn took them away. All Carol could find was a pile of dirt. A dollop of dirt splattered onto the casket making a loud splat!

"Here is to our friendship, I wanted it to have been rose petals," Carol said quietly. "Sorry Pat."

~

That wasn't rose petals that I heard. Sure sounds like mud, Carol. I'm in my casket now. That wasn't nice.

Carol, you could save my life sweetie. I'm not dead. Now really save my life. Come on one more time... Please.

I'm feeling weak again. I need to find that tube. I can't breathe very well.

Help me Carol. Don't throw dirt. Behave Carol. Listen to me. That is so rude.

Hey Carol, Hey Frank, Hey somebody! Help! My finger won't reach the side of the casket.

I'm okay everybody. Why can't they hear me?

I'm at my own funeral. Oh my God!

You can't hear me? Why can't you hear me? It's so hard to speak. Where's my bell? Why can't I reach it? That was supposed to be the point, wasn't it? In case anything like this happened, I could alert someone to help me.

I refuse to die! Somebody filed my nails down. They won't make any sound that way.

Pfft...Pfft...puhfft.

Now my finger hurts. That one finger is missing part of the nail.

Owww!

I can't breathe very well either. This air tube sucks. Help me, somebody. Please?

~

The casket is on a trolley that is next to the hole that was dug. Throwing dirt on it was not appropriate. Frank looked at Carol. "Why did you do that? It wasn't even over the hole."

Carol felt bad. "I didn't mean to do that," she said out loud. Carol retrieved a tissue from her purse and wiped the dirt off her hands. "I'm sorry," she said quietly, *Now they think I'm an idiot*, She said to herself. *Good going Carol, you really did it this time.*

Finnegan began whimpering and got away from Kathryn and yappity barked at the grave. This was not like him. He was acting out and running circles around the casket.

May walked over to Finnegan and picked him up. "Behave! I know your mommy is gone. I miss her too. But you better stop that barking."

The dog became fidgety. He started crying, yapping and whining. He was unlike his normally well behaved self.

May looked at Frank. "Help, look at him, he's uncontrollable. Would you take him?"

~

That's right Finney, I'm in here. Tell them not to bury me. Tell them I'm alive! You're my only hope my sweet, sweet boy. Tell them to get me outta here, right now! Give em hell!

~

Frank scooped up Finnegan from May's arms. Finney had become unmanageable and would not stop barking at the casket.

Carol backed away. "Awww, it's like he knows where Pat is right now. Poor boy, he misses her."

Frank looked at Finnegan and loaded him in his little doggie carriage which looked like a baby stroller. He slowly relaxed, and the stroller quelled him down like he had submitted to that good ole 'doggy role'. His carriage has always been a calming place.

Carol said, "That carriage is so darn cute."

Frank held his hand up to the folks that had congregated for the funeral. "Before I finish up here, I want to invite anyone who would like to join the family at my niece May's house for a bite to eat. It's not much; just finger food. If you need directions my wife Kathryn has a few handwritten maps directing you to the house. I've put them on this table. Thank you all for coming."

It was starting to sprinkle rain when everyone began leaving. Carol said good bye and if May was serious she would be home by two p.m.

2:00 p.m., the same day

A quick rain shower covered the cemetery. Later the sun came out and warmed up the day. It was now a pleasant backdrop for visitors and they were arriving.

Carol wasn't in her house very long when her doorbell rang. It was May and Finnegan.

Wanda had given Carol a call. She said, "I've got to go Wanda, May is here. She has a caravan of boxes and of course Finnegan. She also brought in his carriage." She hung up from her call and opened the door. "Come right in."

May very hurriedly brought in three boxes. It almost looked like someone was arriving to stay for a long time. "I'm sorry about the short notice, but along with my mother dying, and having the wake at my house, my daughter just broke up with her boyfriend that she's had for the past year. I still have visitors at my house.

Finnegan was not behaving. Michelle's prom is tomorrow.

"Anyway, Michelle's found a new boyfriend. Michael Corso, who has invited her to the prom. But unfortunately, Larry keeps calling her and just a few minutes ago he called me. He's a mess. I can't take all the drama. I need to be able to grieve for my poor mother. Anyway, there's a reason for all these boxes. My mother treated Finnegan like her child, as you can see."

May entered Carol's house and handed Finnegan's leash to Carol. "She pointed to the boxes." They are mostly clothes.

"I remember your comment at the funeral Carol. I want to thank you from the bottom of my heart. The family couldn't be more grateful."

May pated Finney. "Here's your boy!"

Carol stood holding Finnegan's leash and staring at May.

"Here's his double bowl, one for water and one for food. Mom gave him dry kibble and sometimes a special treat dog food if he finished his kibble. But he always needs water. Also here is his brush, and his tooth brush. She also buys him these greenies that helps keep the tartar off his teeth. Oh, and here are all his papers for the past eight years worth of vet visits and doggy grooming. His little coats are in those boxes. He has quite the wardrobe. Oh, and here is a pack of coupons that Mom kept when she shopped for his food.

"Any questions Carol?"

Carol stood straight with her cane in hand and smiled ear to ear. "Well, at the moment, no. I just want to say 'Welcome Finnegan!'"

May gave Carol a list of instructions that Pat had given May when she went away on vacation last year. It explained Finney's quirks and his total care card from morning to night. It was a complete schedule. It described how much food, when he can have a treat. There was even a name of a friendly neighborhood dog walker and a friendly dog that Finnegan got along with wonderfully. It was complete, and very detailed.

May said she never read it, but Carol was more than curious.

"Thank you May. I'll take good care of your mother's baby. You can be sure of that."

May smiled, thanked Carol, and left rather quickly. Then she stuck her head back in Carol's house. "Oh, if you want to come over, feel free. I have small petites, little sandwiches and macaroni salad. Oh, and fruit."

"No, I think I should just stay here with Finnegan. We have to get acquainted. Thanks."

May left as quickly as she arrived.

After looking at the list, Carol realized it was getting close to Finnegan's walk time, so she hitched him to his leash and decided to walk over to the cemetery, cane in hand. This was pretty simple. She thought May had delivered the dog rather hurriedly.

3:00 p.m., the same day

Tap, tap...
Maybe one more time.
Tap, tap... Screech...
Oh damn! It's not working. My finger hurts. Oh my! But the voices are back. Wait!
Blowing... Blowing... Big blow!!
I'm here! Well, one thing for sure is I can't talk. Ahem! Why can't I?
Tingaling...aling...aling...
Good, it worked. The bell is working.
Tingaling... Blowing harder. Tingaling...tingaling!
Oh no! The bell! Oh God! It fell! Just great. Now what?
I'm lying out here in the elements. It must have rained. I've been trying to breath in my air tube. It's full of rain and spit.

The bell had broken off of the fastener that her brother Frank had carefully attached to the inside of the casket.

The bell was wedged in between Pat and the side of her casket. It was out of reach of her hand.

The cemetery was a beautiful sight. April brought buds and leaves to all the well manicured trees and shrubs. Visitors had come to see the pristine grounds and walk the path that was said to be two miles up and back. Today the cemetery was active with visitors. The earlier rain didn't seem to hinder the amount of visitors. It seemed to be livelier than usual for a cemetery. Joggers and bicyclists were taking advantage of the warm temperatures. They were scattered about.

Until Pat died, Carol, who lived just next door from the cemetery, had not visited it for the past fifteen years. She had never before set foot there, until Pat's funeral.

Deer Path Cemetery's entrance alone was magnificent. Two four foot stone columns topped with a stone buck's head on one side and a doe's head on the other. Two crabapple trees were right behind the columns and flanked the entrance in full grandeur. The trees were in bloom. They swayed in the warm breeze. The rain covered flowers sprayed the visitors, dropping on everyone as they entered, like being blessed with petals.

"Did you hear something, like a jingle bell?" Carol whispered to Finnegan the poodle?

She didn't remember having walked a dog as far as she had gone.

"Oh... That's right... You're deaf too, aren't you? This is a beautiful place to walk. We're going to do this often. We're going to have a great time Finney."

She walked on, pulling him away from the open, newly dug grave. The ground was damp from the earlier rain shower. Finnegan sniffed the ground feverishly. A grounds keeper rode by on a mower and drowned out the faint sound made by the bell.

"Come on... You're misbehaving... Finnegan, Stop!" He continued to pull. "I had no idea you'd be such a challenge."

Carol's shoulder length, coifed blonde locks were as golden as a palomino. And she pranced around like one, but with a limp. If it hadn't been for her knee injury she would have had more of a bounce in her step. She was steadying along pretty well, adding a cane to her gait. Her figure hadn't changed in ten years. She was still slim and trim and was considered pretty as a picture.

Carol had received some help in the past from a knife or two. She was in her mid fifties and she wore way too much makeup.

Carol Rose loved her maiden name so much that when she married her first husband, Robert Bland, she wouldn't change her name to Bland. When she and Robert divorced and she married her second husband, Charles Gross, who has since died from a heart attack, she again refused to change her last name. How could she call herself Carol Gross? So... It goes, Carol Rose.

When Charley died, Carol's last husband, she was back in the saddle flirting and dating in no time. She always had plenty of men friends that doted on her... For a short while anyway.

Carol was showing signs of bossiness and bitterness toward some of her friends, possibly due to the change of life, they thought. Or maybe she didn't like living alone. In the past she seemed to need someone to take care of her. According to many of her friends and acquaintances, she had become overbearing and drove many of her friends away, especially for the way she had mistreated Pat.

She had lived across the street from Pat and they were close for many years. They visited each other almost on a daily basis. But their relationship changed one day when Carol noticed Pat was in serious pain in her back from a recent fall while walking Finnegan. So Carol said she would help with Finnegan and showed an interest in walking the sweet poodle. Although Pat was a bit reluctant, she didn't question her long time friend. She had not experienced that type of treatment from Carol before. In fact she thought this was way too nice of her.

When Carol arrived back at Pat's house without the dog, she cried, "Poor Finnegan, a stray dog ran up and began chasing both of us. Finnegan pulled away so hard that I lost control of him. He ran away!"

The miniature poodle ran away, with Carol in pursuit? That was simply preposterous. All twelve pounds of Finnegan was getting too old to run away. Besides, he adored Pat and would have run home.

The truth was, Carol believed that Pat was getting too sick and old to be caring for Finnegan. He was peeing on her beautiful hardwood floors. Also, he was starting to limp, showing signs of arthritis himself, and he needed expensive pain relief. Carol regularly blurted out what she thought was best for Pat. And caring for an old, needy, aging dog was not in her best interest. So she had actually surrendered Finnegan to the shelter and concocted the story to tell Pat. She thought she was helping her.

Well, The cat was out of the bag when a local police officer who knew Pat recognized Finnegan while visiting the shelter. He made a special trip to Pat's house and revealed the story to Pat. He brought Finnegan home.

So began the feud.

Patricia Faros was now 'Eligible for Medicare' years old, and up until two days ago had been in perfect health. She had suffered breast cancer once but was in remission for the past five years. She looked younger than her age. She sure didn't look sick. She'd had a bout of arthritis from time to time, but for the most part she was in pretty good health.

She was lucky to have had a full head of shoulder length ash blonde hair. Well, that's what color was revealed on the box of hair color she used. Her figure was still shapely and her personality and smile was what drew you in and made you want to be around her. She was very artistic and was known to give lessons in water color to a handful of friends. Mostly her friends wanted Pat to paint landscapes or still life type paintings for them. They didn't really want the lessons.

When Pat died it upset the whole neighborhood. Everyone came out of the woodwork to get the final determination of how she died. Gossip in that quadrant of town was common.

She left behind Finnegan, her sweet dog of thirteen years. She thought confidently he would have been living with her daughter May, but May never liked Finnegan and didn't have time in her life for a dog. May's sweet Butter Cup, a beautiful orange female tabby cat, didn't want anything to do with a dog either. So ironically, May dropped him off at Carol's house right after the funeral. Imagine! At Carol's house. By then Carol gave in and said she would be honored to have Finnegan. Honored?

Hours after Carol had unexpectedly laid claim to Finnegan at the funeral she was walking him all around the beautiful cemetery. Who would have thought? This was retribution, and so far, not so bad. Carol was having a 'so far... so good' kind of day. Maybe having a dog wasn't so bad after all.

"Oh my," she said, "There is George's grave, with plastic flowers, right next door. Who uses plastic flowers?" she asked herself quietly.

Addressing Pat's casket she said, "You must be so happy."

Carol teared up and blew her nose. She stood up straight holding on to her cane with one hand and Finnegan with the other. A slight chill was left in the air from the recent rain shower, but it wasn't too bad.

She looked at the casket and then at Pat's gravesite. "Good thing I wore a sweater," she said to whoever could hear her.

Carol's knee was still in pain and she was feeling it just from the simple half mile walk.

Carol was regretting not reconnecting with Pat. She was grappling with the loss of her once good friend, especially since she hadn't had a chance to have the talk with her. An apology for her past high jinks. After finding her friend deceased in her dining room, she wasn't able to sleep last night. Well maybe taking care of Pat's dog might give her a bit of comfort. Or at least that is what she was hoping for. But she wanted to mend her relationship with Pat. Now she won't have a chance to apologize to her.

"Pat, I'm here with your baby, Finnegan." She began to fold her hands as in prayer.

~

I hear you Carol. So you have my boy, huh? You better take good care of him. I can't imagine why May gave him up so quickly, and to you, of all people. You're not a dog person. I thought she liked him a little bit anyway. Maybe not though.

Carol, please don't pull any stunts with my sweet dog. I need to get out of here and take Finnegan home with me, once and for all.

Well, I will say Carol, you've come through more than once. I have to thank you. I don't know what would have happened if you didn't find me. Thank you for staying with May during this trying time. Bravo!

The question is, can you really take care of Finnegan? All I can do is pray all goes well. If you take care of Finnegan with the love he deserves you are very special and I take back all the mean things I said about you.

~

"I'm so, so sorry, Pat. You know I will take good care of your angel."

Finnegan pulled hard. He began digging at the dirt.

"Stop!" Carol exclaimed, while pulling him away.

"Pat, I am so sorry. Finney. Stop sweetie! We didn't have a truce before this. Now it's unfixable. You know how much I loved you. I have started and restarted to write you a letter of apology for everything. And now this... Look... Of course you can't. I have Finney, your boy!"

She tugged on Finney's leash as he was becoming more animated and out of control. His leash has now wrapped around her sore leg.

"Oh no!" Carol gasped as she lost her grip on Finnegan's leash.

He took off. Her cane went flying past her reach. Finnegan darted to the adjacent grave and he crouched, assuming the obvious position.

"No, Finney! What are you doing!? Don't do it... On George's grave!"

~

Finnegan what are you doing? Carol is trying to take care of you. Now be a good dog and start barking to let her know I'm alive.

Carol you better take good care of my boy. I love that dog.

Well, well, May didn't let any grass grow under her feet. Did she?

Carol, Finnegan is telling you something. Listen to the dog. I can't believe I'm saying those words. Finnegan knows I'm alive. He's as smart as they come.

Finnegan, come to mommy.

~

As she attempted to reach the dog, Carol lost her balance and toppled over slowly.

"Oh damn! Don't do it." But she's too late and Finnegan left George a special gift.

"Sorry Pat. That's just great Finnegan!" She whispered aloud "Come here!"

She scooted on the grass to reach her cane. As she attempted to get upright she found herself struggling with her cane for support. Her white sweater was now stained from the fresh red clay mud.

~

Now Finney, why knock her down? We don't want anything to happen to her. She's been chosen to take care of you. You have to treat her better than that.

If you poo-pooed on Daddy's grave, that's fine, he wouldn't mind.

Just run around and bark like crazy now and help... And get me outta here. Come on now, get up Carol. I hope you're okay.

Had she known what she was to learn about George she would have praised Finnegan for what he did.

~

Finnegan wandered back over to the tall pile of topsoil by Pat's grave and began darting back and forth around the open grave, barking frantically. He began whimpering and digging in the dirt.

Pat's casket was sitting on a coffin trolley. It's been over four hours since the funeral. The casket was still sitting out in the elements. A rainstorm had just past, making all the dirt wet and muddy.

The rain didn't hurt the casket. It's impervious to rain. But everyone wanted to see the casket six feet under. It was a lovely sunny April day. The rain seemed to be trying to ruin it. Everyone assumed she would have been in the ground by now. The latest information was there were only a few diggers working due to sickness or a supposed flu that had caused a backup of burials today.

Carol fought her way upright and brushed herself off. "Oh dear God, Finnegan, look at my white angora sweater, it's ruined! Get away from there! It's so muddy here. Why don't they bury you Pat? This is ridiculous. Dirt is everywhere, and now it's on me too."

~

Finnegan, it's me! Stop digging baby boy! Yes! It's me my boy! Finnegan, I'm over here. I'm not in the ground yet... I don't think. I'm here sweet boy. I'm in the casket.

Carol, why in the world would you wear a white angora sweater during a walk with Finnegan? I'll buy you another sweater if I get outta here.

Finnegan is the best dog in the world.

Why don't they bury me? Maybe... That should be a sign. I'm not dead. You're all a bunch of fools.

Sniff...

Am I crying? Do I have tears? No, no, help Carol, Finney! Help me please. I need... What do I need? Nothing. Just rescue me. That's the only thing I ask for. I need nothing.

My God, I think I'm crying tears, real tears.

Pat attempted to push her one sore finger, the only one that has any strength, onto the side of the casket. She could only feel a satin type material. This will never do. A snag from her finger nail caught on the material. She pushed with all the strength she had left. No sound could be heard.

Nancy Davis, a neighbor from two blocks away, walked the cemetery path every day. This was part of her exercise regime. She especially loved the crab apple trees this time of year. They were eye catching.

She appeared to be a true friend of Pat's. Sometimes she would take Pat shopping. But mostly they enjoyed having a cup of tea or coffee and working out all the problems of the world, through conversation.

When Pat was sick with cancer she stopped by and helped her with chores and even fed her husband, George. They had become close except for Nancy's complaints about Wanda, who she liked only on some occasions... Only when and if it benefited her.

The newest complaint was Wanda never wore her hearing aids and usually couldn't hear her. But if you ask Wanda why she doesn't wear them she said when she was outside sometimes she would sweat and cause them to malfunction. Nancy just didn't seem to be very sensitive or forgiving even with that explanation.

Today Nancy invited Wanda to take a walk through the cemetery and visit Pat's burial site. She heard that the diggers were not working and she wanted to see for herself.

Flowers were in abundance. They were everywhere leaving their sweet fragrance to permeate the air around the beautiful casket.

Carol scouted around thinking, while looking at her white tennis shoes getting dirtier by the minute, and a huge splat of mud was on the top of one of them. She thought to herself *Why don't they have sidewalks here? The roads are narrow but not busy with cars. So for all these years I could have walked the cemetery instead of up and down my street, like a fool.*

Carol had only had Finnegan for an hour. She was wondering how complicated this decision to care for him was going to be. He was getting full of mud and she wasn't sure how she was going to get it off. She kept her house spotless.

"I guess I'll just have to give you a bath today Finnegan."

Pat's husband George's tomb stone, sprinkled with colorful plastic flowers, was adjacent to the newly dug grave. Carol hadn't attended George's funeral three years prior as she was out of the country on a cruise.

She limped over to collect Finnegan's unwanted gift. She pretended not to see Nancy and Wanda approaching the grave. She grabbed Finney's leash and started searching for anything resembling a doggy do-do bag or tissue.

"Oh darn it." All she had was that one single slightly used tissue that was rolled up in her pedal pusher pants pocket.

The cemetery seemed to be bustling with visitors now. There was a big sign stating 'Pick up doggy-doo please'.

Finnegan had gone from a snow white, clean cut, French Poodle to a dirty, mangy mutt. Red clay mud was all over his coat. He barked and pulled frantically. Carol scooped up the smear of disgusting filth and got it on her hand and cane. She'd tried hard to get control of the situation when she noticed Wanda, standing nearby.

Carol waved, turned and walked on, to gain control of the dog. She was hiding her recovered poop. She passed both graves and spoke under her breadth to Finnegan.

"You little cur," she said with disgust. "We'll see who goes for a walk after this!" Carol was furious. He was acting like a little devil, she thought.

Carol stomped her cane along with an awkward hopping step, juggling her cane and the leash. She again lost her balance and stumbled. First she dropped, then landed smack on, the filthy tissue. Carol looked around. This was now a living nightmare.

Without hesitation, Bruno, the grounds keeper, came around the corner and jumped off his mower, leaving it idling. He rushed over to Carol and reached down to pull her to her feet. His hand grasped Carol's soiled hand which was now holding the tissue. His gallantry was observed by all.

"Oh... Shit!" Bruno exclaimed. Then, after helping Carol to her feet, he shook his soiled hand in the air and then he began frantically wiping it on the grass.

~

Oh my God! I think someone heard me, but now there's that damn mower. Go away!

Brumm…brumm…brumm...

I'm tapping as loud as I can. Now I'm losing my strength! Oh God...

Pfft...pfft... Screeeech...

Somebody... Help!

The sound of the idling mower is all that could be heard.

Now I'm losing air... Gasp... I can't catch my breath! Gasp...wheeze... Oh... The pain!

I can only move one finger and the nail is getting shorter and shorter. And they'll put me in the ground soon! They have to cover me up with dirt and I don't think I'll make it. Help!

~

"They still haven't buried Pat!" Wanda patted the casket. "Hey there Pat, how's it going?"

~

Is that you Wanda?

~

"Dear God! I think I heard something!"

Because she wasn't wearing her hearing aids, she put her face down close to the casket and strained to hear the sound again.

"Is anyone in there? Hello... Can you hear me?"

She turned to tell Nancy and noticed Carol standing unsteadily after having been helped to her feet by Bruno, who was now on his knees frantically wiping his hands on the grass for some reason.

~

"I am sooo exhausted! I think I can... I think I can... I think I... Can't! Just great! Now I'm either really dead or paralyzed.

*Shoot! Wanda… I hear you but I can't talk. I'm trying,
but I can't tap with this crooked finger anymore. Please…
Please… Don't go away!*

Blow...pfft...pfft!

Wanda, help me!

She managed to make one clear, *tap tap* with her sore
finger.

Ouch!

~

Nancy shook her head at Wanda. "You don't have
your hearing aids on, do you? What are you doing? You
wouldn't be able to hear her if she was singing the Star
Spangled Banner.

"You know I heard Carol hated dogs. Pat told me.
Why is she walking Pat's dog anyway? Wanda! How
embarrassing. Wanda what are you doing? Please get
away from that casket."

~

*You aren't treating Wanda very nice, Nancy. She
really did hear me. You're hindering her. How would you
like to be hard of hearing? And how would you like to be*

in a casket alive and getting ready to be buried? I think you would be devastated!

~

Wanda stood next to the casket and rapped twice gently again with her knuckles. "I'm communicating with Pat, since she was the only one around here that knew it was my birthday."

Nancy sheepishly said, "What? I really didn't know. I'm sorry, it's today, the day of Pat's funeral? Oh Wanda... Happy Birthday."

"Hello Pat. It's me Wanda. Today is my birthday and you and I would be the same age. I'll never forget the day of your funeral. It was perfect. The weather was lovely, the sun was shining. It was on my birthday. It felt like you were actually present... Well you were. But it felt like you knew how perfect the funeral was. But now, I wonder why they haven't buried you yet. I'm going to talk to someone. Don't you worry my friend? I'll talk to Blain today. It's supposed to rain tonight."

~

Wanda... Wanda... Wanda! Thank God you're here. Happy Birthday, my friend Wanda. Save me my friend. Please! I'm alive!

What do you mean 'We would be the same age'? We are the same age. I'm alive! Help me Wanda! Happy Birthday! You're now sixty-five. Terrific!

Well my friend, please rap on my casket again. I'll rap back. Don't listen to Nancy. She's not acting very sensitive toward you today.

~

Nancy looked at her walking buddy making a fool of herself. "Wanda, who are you talking to?"

"I know I heard something. Did you hear a pfam...pfam sound, and some tapping, Nancy? Maybe she's trying to communicate with us."

Nancy shakes her head and slowly starts to walk on.

"Do you suppose Pat's come back because we didn't invite her to our breakfast brunch?" She grinned slightly. "No, really I did hear something. Didn't you hear anything?"

Wanda heads in the direction of Nancy.

"No!"

~

Yes Wanda, you did hear something. It's me! I had no idea you had a breakfast party, brunch or whatever, and although a bit disappointed, I could care less. So let's get past that and listen carefully to me. I need your help. Just find someone to open my casket and save me, please.

~

Nancy said, "In her predicament, she could care less. If she were really alive, knowing her, she would raise cane. She would huff and puff and blow that casket down. Pat was tough. No question."

~

Believe me, I would if I could Nancy. Don't leave! Your voices are fading away. This is reality though and I'm in here and it was a mistake. Why can't you hear me and Wanda can? Nancy can't you hear me?

Pat moves her finger up and down making a softer swoosh...swoosh...pfam...pfam sound.

~

Nancy shook her head, "Wanda you were embarrassing me. Please stay away from that damn casket."

~

What is wrong with you Nancy? Damn casket? Well Wanda heard me, and you're being nasty. Leave her alone. Anyway, it's my casket. It's not damn *at all. Wanda don't leave me.*

~

Nancy looked straight at the casket a bit embarrassed. She thought she heard something, also. "What in the world was that?" She shook her head like it was ridiculous. She began walking away from the casket talking under her breadth. "What the hell did I hear?"

~

See... I know you heard me Nancy. Wanda was right. You just won't admit it.

~

"Wanda, come on! Let's go, I have dinner plans, and this is getting really weird."

"Plans huh? Are you taking me out to dinner, how nice of you?"

"Oh no, I'm sorry. We can do that some other time. It's an old friend of mine. It's no big deal."

"I'm only kidding. I'm going home to have dinner with my neighbors. We've been friends for years. They invited me. We're playing cards afterwards."

Nancy Davis was a fit retired school teacher who walked two miles with her friend Wanda every day, through the picturesque cemetery. They prayed whenever they saw a new burial.

Nancy was the lead in a prayer group that Wanda and Pat belonged to. There were several other girls but attendance was down lately. The group was not functioning at full capacity.

Nancy always had a strange theme and Pat and Wanda didn't always agree with her themes. One week the topic was 'What have you done for your neighbor lately?'. Wanda and Pat thought it was strange. Don't get me wrong. It's right and just to look ahead and have a better understanding of your neighbor. They might be out of work or depressed and can't go to the store. Or... Whatever.

They just wanted to go back to the old way of just taking a psalm in the bible and reviewing it for a better understanding; for its meaning. But the prayer group was important to Nancy, because she was the lead. She had her own course in mind. She wanted to help her community more.

Wanda patted the casket. She said, "See you later my friend."

~

Bye Wanda.

Pat pushed her finger hard two times. It made a scratching sound.

Good.

~

Wanda turned back as she began to walk away. She put her head close to the casket. "What was that? Are you responding to me Pat? I swear I heard something Nancy. Do that again!"

"Wanda, come on, really? Please. You are losing it dear girl!"

She walked on a few steps ahead of Wanda hoping she'd come to her senses. "I'm not stopping. I'm heading home. Bye."

"I know what I heard!" Wanda looked back and fast walked to catch up to Nancy.

Wanda looked straight at Nancy. "If I had worn my hearing aids would you have believed me?"

Nancy shook her head and responded, "Probably not. Come on, let's go!"

Bruno, the handsome mower attendant, drove by. Both women turned their heads his way. Wanda smiled. "Why do you think he is he holding his hand up?"

Wanda said, "Look at him, that poor guy." They both giggled. "Well you're right. We better go."

Nancy made the sign of the cross. "God Bless you." She whispered, "You're loved dear!"

Wanda looked over at Nancy. "She's gone... Too sad... You're right. Let's go home. I'm feeling a little uneasy. I'm afraid she might have heard us." She giggled. "Imagine if she really heard us? "

They walked away. "I'm not kidding. I personally heard something when we first arrived." Wanda snickered. "It's talking to the dead that's eerie. I thought I heard kind of a scratching sound. No bell though, very strange, I'd swear I heard something, like she's not dead yet. Poor, poor dear. I'm going to find that Blain. Why is she out in the elements?"

~

"No... Don't go! I'm alive! I'm a poor, poor dear. You're right. Please don't go Wanda. You're right. I'm not dead... Yet! You said yet. You just said it. Wanda, you're right! But don't find Blain. Now I'm alone and I don't know how to get anyone's attention. Maybe I'll really die now. Wanda!

~

Suddenly A familiar voice was heard.

"Hi Pat. It's me, Diane Price. We were in a prayer group together. I just saw Nancy walk by.

"I just wanted to let you know I'm so upset that you passed. I will pray for you. The group won't be the same you know.

"I was at your funeral today, it was nice. I offered my condolences to your handsome brother Frank.

"Anyway, Nancy and Wanda just walked by and that brought back a weird memory. I don't think they recognized me. I just wanted to say, one day when Nancy finished prayer group early and I went into the parking lot. I saw your husband George sitting in her car. He looked like he was trying to hide from me. I walked behind the building. You were gone. Nobody was in the parking lot. I just live a block away so I could walk. I stood behind the building and when Nancy got in her car, George and Nancy began kissing passionately.

"I couldn't believe it. I didn't know what to do. We had just talked about cleaning house and practicing what we preach. We should be kind to one another and not commit sins against our neighbors. We were talking about making the world a better place.

"I just stood there frozen. Then when I looked back at the parking lot, they were gone.

"I've held this in for three years. I'm sorry I didn't have the nerve to say anything while you were alive. I hope you will forgive me. I should have let you know. I'm sorry. Please forgive me Pat. That's why I dropped out of prayer group.

"I remember when you called me and said you missed me. Well I missed you too. But I just couldn't face you anymore. I didn't want to do this. But I couldn't do it while you were alive. I guess I'm just chicken.

"So that's all I wanted to say to you.

"I'm going to leave now. God Bless your soul. I'm sorry if this upsets you. Try and rest in peace."

~

What? Try and rest in peace? You should have told me right when it happened... If it happened. That's what friends are for Diane. We help each other out. We don't hide secrets when it's the adulterous type. Come on. Friends are for safe keeping. We should cherish each other, not avoid, or run and hide.

Diane, I don't like what you told me. It really hurts, but you did tell me and I appreciate that. Boy oh boy that changes a whole lot. Nancy was one of my best friends. At least you came through.

Nancy was getting on my nerves lately.

Now that we're passed that, get me the hell outta here. I have a bone to pick with some people. I seem to be learning more as a dead person than as an alert living human. I had no clue.

Maybe you're just wrong. Maybe that didn't happen. I would have and should have seen it coming. Or would I? George could be a very curious man. He did vanish often. I just thought he was sneaking food or having a beer or two at the local. Now you have me wondering. Oh well, I guess I'll never know now.

April 15, noon

Rain rain, go away... Please come again some other day... Oh my! It's getting so hard to breathe. Well am I dead or am I dying... Why... Can't I feel anything but one finger? Oh wait my chest is beginning to hurt.

Finnegan, please find me. I am freezing! I'm chilled to the bone. Where is everybody? Oh... Right... Who am I kidding? They're in their warm homes drinking hot tea.

She attempted to suck in more air through the air tube. It got stuck on her tongue.

Bl...ubbba...pffft...

Why aren't I scared anymore? Why am I feeling so weird?

Pfff...pffft...pffft...

Oh... It's oxygen depravity. I will need to be rescued soon because I am not able to breathe anymore. I'm getting water in my air tube.

Blub...blub...pffft.

I wonder what time it is now. Okay goofy, it's raining. Who goes to the cemetery in the rain? Anyway they think your dead. They're in their warm houses, probably in their warm robes, or having a hot cup of tea reading a good book, or watching TV.

I think I'm falling asleep.

My wonderful family. Will I ever see them again?

And you George! I thought we had something special since that night at our prom...

Forty-five years earlier, prom night

Pat Brigham was eighteen and graduation was just around the corner. George Faros had been her boyfriend for the past year.

Ruth, Pat's mother, always trusted her daughter. Pat told her mother there was a chaperone and she and George were headed to the school prom together. From there she, George and several of her friends would be leaving for the Jersey Shore that same evening. They were staying overnight at Bubba's Shack on the beach. It's a slew of motel cabins that are known for spring break.

Ruth didn't worry at all. She trusted everything her daughter told her. Pat was responsible and dating a senior with an Ivy League college in his sights. She felt there was nothing to be concerned about. Pat had never before given Ruth reason to doubt her.

So Pat and friends all left for the prom. Her gown was purple; her favorite color.

Ruth had just lost her husband, Frank Sr., earlier in the year due to a cancer related surgery. He died on the table. Ruth wanted to keep her daughter as happy and secure as possible after a rough year. It was life altering so this was still a difficult time in Ruth's life. She had loved him. He was her soul mate.

Ruth had become very close to her youngest daughter Pat. She was the only child left at home. Ruth was not able to contribute much for the prom or any extra celebrations during Pat's last year in school. Simply because of a small pension; she couldn't afford any extra bills.

Ruth noticed by midsummer her daughter had been putting on weight. It soon became clear that Pat was pregnant.

Her older son, Frank Jr., was newly married and he and his wife were trying desperately to have a child, but Kathryn had an atopic pregnancy and was on her second attempt to get pregnant. The doctors informed Kathryn she would never be able to bare a baby full term.

Pat and George broke off their relationship right before Pat found out she was pregnant. Abortion was not on the table according to Pat. So she kept her new son who she named Beaufort; Bo for short. This was from her great grandfather who Ruth loved. They adored this child.

Life was tough for Ruth. Trying to pay all the bills and add the expense of co-raising a new baby boy.

That's when Ruth came up with the solution. Her son and daughter in law were getting ready to consider adoption. It was like the hand of God came down and placed it on the family. It worked like a charm. Frank, Kathryn, Ruth, and finally Pat all agreed.

Giving up the child to her brother and his wife would be the solution. The child would still be in the family. Pat agreed with some slight hesitation, but knowing she would get to see Bo whenever she wanted was a gift. She would offer her son to her brother and his wife for adoption. Even the child's last name would not have to change. Her last name was Brigham so the baby carried the name.

Three years later Pat was back with her boyfriend George Faros and they were engaged to be married. The engagement lasted one year and it was so exciting because she was marrying her childhood sweetheart.

He was graduating from the Wharton School of Business at the University of Pennsylvania with an MBA. He found a job right away.

There was no mention of the birth of their child. It was a clean slate. George never found out about the baby. Within a year of their marriage they conceived their daughter, May. Bo and May were close as cousins; in reality they were brother and sister

George became very close to Bo. And George was someone that Bo respected a great deal and looked up to in life. They spent a good amount of time together.

So life went on without a hitch.

Pat Faros was extremely happy when they bought a house right down the street from her brother Frank, Kathryn and sweet Bo. Life was working out perfectly so far.

Martha was Pat's older sister and she was sickly most of her life. She didn't marry but had a very lucrative job with the federal government.

Family was everything to her and she became much attached to Bo as well. She always treated him like he was her own child. She bought him things and took him to museums, baseball games and taught him to knit.

When May was born she divided much of her attention between them both. Unfortunately Martha was sick with MS for many years. She eventually became blind and finally succumbed due to a chronic related infection. Martha left Bo and May most of her estate. The rest went to MS research.

April 15, 3:30 p.m.

The temperature was an almost balmy seventy-two degrees. The son had peeked from the big puffy cumulous clouds that had opened up from a recent rain shower.

Barbara Stetson, a close friend of Pat and George's, walked up to the casket. Of the people she knew, Barbara was one of Pat's favorites. She and her husband Paul planned and went on cruises with Pat and George. They enjoyed each other's company. Twice a month they went out to dinner together. Card night with tacos was Friday nights. But Pat hadn't seen them since George died suddenly three years ago.

Barbara was standing at Pat's casket with a happy face vase filled with daises. "I apologize Pat, for not making your funeral. Ewww, it's all soggy here. It must have rained pretty hard. Anyway, Paul and I had an argument. This turned into a migraine headache and I couldn't get out of bed. And to think he accused me of having an affair with George. Go figure. Well what if it was true? You're both gone and we're all adults. I can't see why it's such a biggie.

"Anyway Pat, I made it. Hello my friend. I'm so sorry I missed your funeral today, but here I am now. Perky as the daises I brought you. I'll set them on the ground so as not to disturb all the other flowers that surround you."

~

Oh Barbara, hello. There you are. Such a biggie, is that what you said? Biggie, huh? Are you kidding me? What exactly do you mean... Not a biggie... Huh?

~

"Anyway, Pat I've wanted to have a talk with you about a matter that now cannot wait. That cruise we went on about four years ago to Aruba, do you remember? You were not feeling well so you went into your cabin. My Paul was sea sick and he went in our cabin. Well... That day I spent the day with your George. Well... We had an affair in one of the empty rooms that was open. We were having so much fun and drank way too much and the rest is history.

"Well... That was the beginning of many clandestine moments together. These three years without your George have been difficult for me; as for you I'm sure. But I'm feeling better now and my Paul and I have revitalized our own relationship. I was getting ready to

contact you. Well... As life happens you're now gone...
So here we are."

~

I was *wishing I could hug you. I have been thinking
about you for the past three years. Now I know why
you've been AWOL... You were doing the dirty with
George. You must have felt mighty guilty because it was
like you fell off the face of the earth. Where have you
been? Now that George is gone, I guess I was too.*

*A four letter word for dead. That could be it, **gone**.
You squirming worm. You had to wait until I died. Until I
was gone. Or at least you think I'm dead. You're
spineless. How could you Barbara? Couldn't you have
just had some fun? Why did you ruin a long term
relationship? Oh don't get me wrong. My husband was
every bit as wrong as you. But you were my close friend...
How could you? I'll deal with him later. But you... I don't
get it!*

~

Suddenly, Barbara thought she recognized someone walking along the path at the cemetery so she quickly said, "Bye Pat." She gave the casket a tap tap and left.

~

Don't you dare leave without some kind of explanation. Well I guess we're done girl. Please do leave. I don't want to hear your voice again... Unless you can get me out of this predicament.

~

Just moments following Barbara's departure a younger woman approached the casket.

A pretty, middle aged brunette, stood at George's grave holding two white roses. She bent down and placed one on George's grave.

She said very quietly, "Hello again George, it's me. You know who, Kitten. I haven't stopped by in a while. Sorry. After I heard about your wife, I couldn't stay away. I just want to say I still love you George. I can honestly say that I have a feeling of relief now. My feelings for you have not wavered one bit, since that day at the cabin in the woods. I've had dreams about that place, to this day. I know if it wasn't for my flat tire, I would have never met you. Our twenty year age difference didn't mean anything to me or you. You were so kind. Right then I knew. You were too good to be true, and you were the one for me.

"Well, I just want you to know I'm still not married. I probably will never marry. You will be on my mind forever. That guy I told you I was dating, Marty, well he gave up on me. He said he didn't want to vie for my attention with a corpse."

~

Pat almost jumped out of her casket.

What... Who is that?

She tried to recognize the voice but she couldn't, no matter how hard she tried.

Wanda? No... Nancy? No... Who could it, be? Is this the girl from the bank? No... You sound too old to be Marci. Oh my God! Kitten huh? So George, who is Kitten? Not our cabin... Was it? You wouldn't George.

Now I remember reading a piece of note paper in your shorts. It had a phone number on it, with the name kitten. I thought it was about the kitten you said you found. George, you said you found a kitten and called a couple places and got a phone number and found the owner of the kitten. Shrewd idea there George... But when did this happen? Not on our anniversary I hope.

Now I remember... You helped someone with a flat tire on that same day. I remember when you said you found a kitten at the cabin when you went fishing. That's the missing puzzle piece. It's making sense now, more like nonsense. As mad as I am about Kitten, I fell for it then, hook, line and sinker. It was an adorable story that pisses me off now. You said you found the owner of the poor kitten. You dirty rat, George, especially since it was our anniversary. You came home so late. But after you told me the story that was sewed to the last fragments of an excuse I believed you and I've told the story to so many people. Now it's all making sense. Now I can't breathe. The lie was on our anniversary. George... What have you done?

Suddenly her charley horse came back and her foot bumped the side of the casket causing the bell to ding-a-ling.

~

Kitten jumped.

"What the hell was that? Oh my God! She must be alive!

"I'm so, so sorry Patricia, this was meant to be. I believe you heard me and in your way, you have acknowledged my existence. This had to happen I'm sure. Namaste my new friend."

Kitten left the other rose that was in her hand on the top of her casket. She prayed, then said, "Good bye Patricia, George told me many good things about you. You were a very lucky woman. I know, because he's changed my life forever."

She left walking quickly away wondering if this was a good or bad omen. Then she saw someone heading toward the casket.

~

George, what in God's name did you do with that woman? I should say those women? You made Kitten heartsick. But George, we had a wonderful anniversary dinner that evening with the Stetson's. Paul and Barbara Stetson brought over a full course meal to our house for our anniversary, remember? Barbara was so sneaky. How could you be so nonchalant about having an affair with her? Especially having a tryst on our anniversary, George.

We had fun that night. Remember. We had a bottle of wine; Barbara made a delicious German chocolate cake that was out of this world. I'm sure you and Barbara were on the porch making out while I cooked our dinner that night. That was one of the most memorable nights since our wedding. I thought. You must be a real stallion Georgie boy. You made me feel like I was the only woman in the world. Well I was one of the only clueless fools in the world, wasn't I? How blind could I be?

Now how am I supposed to feel? Reality has just sunk in. I'm in this casket and you... You're probably wining and dining with the devils concubine. With who knows who?

You always came back to me though, I'll give you that. You loved me more than any of them. But somehow that's not enough George. I don't want to have anything to do with you anymore.

How did you find the time? Stay out of my dreams from now on. My heart is broken enough. For three years I could hardly get out of bed because of you.

If I get outta here, no one will ever know the truth. I can barely believe it myself. But I will not taint our family, ever! I love my family more than ever now. No one will ever hurt my family. And the good news is, I now know who I can and can't trust. I now know who my real friends are. So for that George, I thank you.

~

"Hello Mommy."

May walked up to the casket that is still just next to the hole. She picked up the rose and smelled it.

"Wow, this is beautiful and smells so fragrant. So many people must have loved you Mommy. The daisies are so refreshing.

"Mommy, Michelle has a new boyfriend. He's smart, really nice, and polite and not to mention handsome as all get out. Larry's out!"

~

Nice, good. I like Larry, but he was a bit of a dummy when he took his driver's test and crashed into the state trooper's car. Larry was too immature for Michelle.

Now I remember why I didn't like Larry. He took her with two other friends to the state park and brought alcohol, getting her so drunk she passed out. That was a stupid move. When they left all their empty beer cans next to the trash can at the state park. They just ran out of beer. That was when she came to my house for my help. She said Larry peed in your car, May, when she drove him home. I tried to get the smell out. But Golly May, that was ridiculous. You even tried but couldn't get the smell out of the car for days. Remember? Oh sure he apologized. But Michelle is better off without a knucklehead like him.

The only good thing that boy did was give me that whistle, that I can't quite reach.

Refreshing... The flowers are refreshing alright. More like earth shattering.

She started feeling sleepy. She started counting silently.

One, two... Oh God!... Three. Oh God... I don't want to fall asleep. Why am I feeling this way? I must be hallucinating. I feel like I'm floating. Maybe I'm dying for real. It's all because of you George.

May, I can't talk to you yet. I'm trying to get over the latest garbage about your father. No one would believe what your father did. What have you done to me George... To our marriage?

I can hear but can barely move. My fingers are so sore. My strength is gone. I can't give up now.

Oh May, my sweet daughter. Help me. I might really be dying now. We won't talk about your father ever again. He's pulled a doozey. I'm so glad you're here now. But I'm lethargic and I'm afraid I will fall asleep soon.

~

"Mommy."

May never called her mother 'Mommy' before, But she had on numerous occasions this past two days. "I love you. And I always will.

"Mom, I just want to say I'm sorry for being a problem child. Especially for giving pot to Finnegan that time I was 'Finney sitting' for you. But Mom, he wouldn't stop barking at my cats, Butter Cup and Tuxedo. When I took care of him last year he was so naughty he chased poor Tux all over the house. Butter Cup hid for the whole time he was there.

"I would not have given Finney a good life if I kept him. He would have had to live outdoors most of the time. Carol said she would love to have Finnegan."

~

Pat was fuming, her tired state completely changed. She was abruptly awakened.. She was thinking that May must have kept Finnegan outside in the rain the week she went to Florida.

Great... Just great! Now you tell me. How could you do that? You're deceitful just like your father. Well... Not THAT bad. I guess you just didn't want anything to do with him. My own fault dear. I forced Finnegan on you. Sorry. No problem. Really May. I love you my dear girl.

I'll always love you till my dying day... Oh that may be right now.

Okay May... Glad you told me. Now, get me out of here my sweet girl. Please May. Okay, okay, I forgive you... But pot? What happened to Finnegan. Did he get sick? Did he stay outside the whole time I was gone? Well I guess that was the best you could do. I love Finnegan. I can't expect anyone to love him as much as me. That doesn't change how I feel about you. Sure I wish you didn't do that to my poor Finney but he looked healthy and happy when I came home from vacation and I spoiled him ever since.

So... Now that we've settled that get me out of here! It's your father that betrayed me. Not you. I miss you May. I miss Michelle too. Kiss her for me.

~

"Anyway, Carol will give him a good home, Mom. Oh, I heard about that day she took Finney to the pound. But Carol loved you. You know that. You were suffering so much back pain at the time she didn't know what to do for you. I'm sure she would do anything for you, she loved you and her very words when you died were 'I would take Finnegan in a heartbeat!'. Well she came through. She seemed to be getting along with him just fine.

"Mom, I wish you weren't in there. I need this to be a nightmare. It doesn't seem real. I miss you so much. I miss just stopping by your house and having a great cup of coffee and helping finish your crossword puzzle. I remembered that one puzzle we couldn't figure out the day you passed. That word we were messed up but I figured it out. It was the three letter word for poke. It was easy, 'jab'. I figured it out when I hung up the phone.

"Anyway, I love you. I'll pray for you. So there you have it. I'm going home now... Kisses."

~

'Jab'... Oh that's right, you are right.

Wait... get me outta here. If you miss me so much, pray they get me outta here! Wait!

Pat attempted to tap the coffin but her nail was too short. It didn't make much sound.

Don't leave May. What about me? Please save me. I'm SO scared. Don't go May, my sweet daughter. Help. Save me! I don't want to end up where your father is, because I might kill him. How could you George?

She tried again, but a soft 'tap tap' is all she had left. Her energy was beginning to wane.

~

May turned around when she thought she saw Mark, the handy man, attempting to hide behind someone standing nearby. "Hi Mark," she said in a friendly manner.

Embarrassed, he walked over and said, "Hello May. I'm just checking on your mother." Then he sheepishly asked, "Why haven't they buried her?"

"It's the pits, isn't it?" May said, holding back tears. "Something about a flu going around and the diggers are all sick. You know she wasn't embalmed yet. This was not at all part of the plan."

"This is not right. I'm going to find the owner," Mark said, as he looked intently at May. "I am so, so sorry for your loss, dear."

He bowed his head and said a prayer under his breath. "God bless this wonderful woman and keep her in your arms. Amen."

May smiled at Mark and said, "Amen."

She was thinking how nice Mark seemed and she felt guilty for being rude to him in the past. She was seeing the side of him that Pat was attached to.

~

"No Mark, don't find the owner. He'll have me buried. Find me! I'm dying Mark, save me, please.

Pat picked with her finger and created a stronger 'tap tap', louder than ever before.

People that have visited me are going to send me too my grave. Help me Mark.

~

"Did you hear that?" May stood with her mouth open. May looked at the coffin and then at Mark.

Mark hadn't heard what May heard. He walked closer to the casket since he had stepped back a few feet to let May talk privately to her mother.

"I don't hear anything."

Mark was hard of hearing and not wearing his hearing aids, he looked quizzically at May. "Hear what? What did it sound like?"

~

Yes, my dear girl. You heard right! Damn it Mark, I'll bet you don't have your hearing aids on, do you? If I ever get outta here, you'll hear me alright! I'll buy you new hearing aids.

~

May cried softly and said her goodbyes again. "Bye Mom! I must be losing it. I thought I heard something coming from your casket. Your spell is on me Mommy. Well, she didn't ring the bell..." She laughed.

"Bye!" May waved at Mark as she began to leave.

She heard Michelle walking down the path talking on her cell phone to her ex-boyfriend Larry.

"No Larry, you can't tell me what to do anymore. ... Michael and I are going to the prom and that's that. ... I'm sorry you aren't going now. That's not my fault. We broke up a month ago. ... You had plenty of time to find someone to go with. Stay home with your weird friends. I'm sure they aren't going.

... "Stop it. Don't call me or my mother again. It's over. Get it? We're not a couple anymore." She hung up and stared at her mother and shook her head.

"Hi Mom. He's thick. He won't accept we're not a couple anymore. I'm going home to get dressed soon. If you see him, don't say a word to him. It has nothing to do with you. Okay?"

May said to her daughter, "I like the way the hairdresser pulled all that hair up high in a bun and left a couple curls cascading. That looks so pretty. You will be simply beautiful."

"Thanks Mom. Larry is being such a pain right now. You wouldn't believe it."

"Don't talk to him. It only makes you angry. He probably just loves you. He can't help it. You're one of the prettiest girls at school. He'll be okay, don't worry about him."

"I'm not worried about him. I'm worried about Michael's and my privacy. He's been bugging Michael.

"Mom, you shouldn't be here. It's not good for you. You need to go home."

Michelle addressed her grandma in the coffin, "Hi Nan, I miss you. Your daughter can't seem to leave. She's here more than she's home, and tonight's the prom. Somehow I wish you would tell her to go home."

Suddenly, Finnegan came yappity barking and running around the casket.

~

Tap tap…screech screech…tap…tappity tap.

Hearing her dog Finnegan gave Pat a boost. With all her might she began tapping and scratching with her middle and pointer finger. She scratched as hard as she could.

Finnegan, I knew you'd come back!
Tap…tap…tap…tap.

~

Michelle picked Finnegan up and said, "What are you doing here? Mom, will you take you over to Carol's house. I'm not going to have time."

~

Finnegan! Hello my sweet dog. You are the only one that knows I'm in this casket alive. You know your mommy isn't dead. But no one will listen to you.

~

"Miss Michelle! Don't tell Nan Finnegan's loose again. We don't want to tell her about our problems. She has enough to worry about. I'm going home now, I'll drop him off at Carol's."

"How did you get here?"

Michelle handed Finnegan to her mother.

"Larry picked me up. But, it wasn't planned. He saw me walking and picked me up. I said thanks. Then he actually begged that I go back with him. Never in a million years would that happen.

"I was at Nan's house across the street. Uncle Frank was going through her things and I wanted to make sure my stuffed animals would still be there.

"So Larry gave me a ride. It's not far and I shouldn't have accepted a ride with him. Now he's a lost cause. He won't leave me alone. We're hours away from the prom, and I'm not going to have all that stress. I'll never ask him for any more favors.

"He had a guy in the car I couldn't stand; I think his name was Scott. He was making weird noises in the car, like a cat. He's a sicko anyway. I can't stand Larry anymore either. He's a loser. He thought he owned me.

"Anyway, I gotta go. Bye Mom... Bye Nan... Bye Finnegan!"

Michelle waved to Mark and put a note on Pat's casket. It read: I will always love you Nan.

"Let's go Mom. You have to leave too."

They both left. May started softly crying and holding onto her daughter's arm, holding Finnegan with the other arm.

~

No... Don't go May! Rescue me! I'm alive. The bell fell. I need to get outta here. Mark are you still here? I miss you. Don't you leave me too! Please. Somebody, help me right now. Michelle, don't go. I'm alive. May, Michelle, Mark!

~

Mark stood back close to the grave shaking his head. "Bye, Pat. I would have liked it if we could have been more than just friends. I'll miss you. I love you Pat."

~

You said you loved me. That is so sweet. My husband was a traitor. He was a wolf in sheep's clothing. He's not on my mind like he once was. Mark, you are on my mind now. I need to talk to you Mark. If you get me out of here, I'll make up for all the lost time. Please help me. Don't go.

She pushed with her foot, making a soft tap.

I love you too Mark.

~

"What in the world?

"I better go home and get some sleep Pat. I haven't been able to sleep since you died. Now I'm hearing things. I guess I'm hallucinating.

"Bye sweet girl.

"Oh by the way, I bought you a friendship necklace with a heart. I was going to give it to you on your birthday but I was chicken. I think I'll keep it to remember you by. Kisses." He walked away toward his truck.

He passed by Laurie Shepherd who was a long time friend of Pat's. She was married to Bill, an old high school boyfriend of Pat's. Laurie was also a book club member with Pat. They often exchanged favorite books. Laurie's husband was in love with Pat once in high school. But that was long before George and the marriage.

~

No Mark, don't go! I want to see the necklace. Please don't go. You heard me. I know you did. I had no idea just how sweet you really were. Now you've proven it. Save me! Don't complain to Blain. I don't want to be buried yet... I mean ever. Please save me.

Pfft...Pfft. Screech!

Good, maybe you heard it.

~

"Hello Pat. It's me Laurie. You know, Laurie Shepherd.

"Remember that last book I shared with you, 'A Heart Divided'? I guess I needed to vent today. That was me; you know the main character, Bella, who had an affair with her best friend's husband. Well that's what happened between George and me. We really did love each other.

"Remember when you forced George to drive me home that night of the fondue? My car wouldn't start. He tried to give me a jump." She giggled.

"I mean he tried to jump my car but it wouldn't turn over. Well... When he drove me home I became Bella in the book. I just fell wildly in love with him. He knows how to treat a lady. He kissed my neck. That's what started this whole affair.

"I'm so sorry Pat. George is the reason I quit the book club. We were so much in love. Or at least I was so much in love. I couldn't face you anymore. I knew all along how wrong it was.

"George tried to break it off so many times. He said he was too much in love with you to change his life for me. Oh, not to mention my sneaking around on Bill. Bill told me once he used to love you before George came into the picture. All the men gravitated to you. You were so lucky. He said he had a fight with George over you back in senior year. George gave him a shiner.

"Well... I want you to know our affair didn't last too long. Oh, we snuck around right after graduation but not for long. George gravitated to you. It wasn't until three

years ago that we struck up a new flame. I swear. Maybe
we were lovers a handful of times. I know that it was
important to me to tell you my friend. It didn't last too
long."

~

*Well, well, well if it isn't Laurie the lady, I mean the
tramp. It didn't last too long huh? That's an interesting
little story if you ask me. So you only had a handful.
Humph. Do you mean when you were fooling around he
was a handful or... When you were holding him he was a
real handful? Either way Laurie, I won the prize. He
didn't leave me for you.*

*You imbecile! So you must be reading too many love
triangles and confessions. I wouldn't recommend them.
Why don't you go confess this very story to Bill, your
sweet husband?*

*You better hope I never get out of here. That would
make a cover story for True Confessions. Now that would
be a good book to read. Whatever it is he would say. That
would be the confession that would be appropriate right
about now. Tell Bill! Ask him what he thinks of you after
you tell him.*

*Look at me. I'm in a casket ready to be buried. So I
guess you feel safe. You can tell me anything. Well
Laurie, guess what? Although I am not a violent person,
I'm not a dead person either, and when I get out, I'm*

*going straight after that fake pony tail you've been wearing...**friend**...!*

You don't realize that what you just did was to try and put a nail in my coffin. I'll get outta here. You'll see.

I'm feeling weak now.

Why would George do that? George, if you can hear me... Why? What was wrong with our relationship? I thought we had it all. I thought ours was perfect.

Well... Laurie you gave me a different perspective on my marriage. It sucked, now I know, so thanks! Go talk to George. You two were made for each other.

~

"George, so, I told her. I feel so much better. It's like a weight off my shoulders. Oh, wow, I feel *so* much better. I hope you're not rolling over in your grave, George. You know I had to do this. She deserved it."

Laurie walked closer to George's grave.

"George, I'm sorry but I had to tell Pat. It was only right. It's important she know. I know we both made a promise. Don't be mad, because I believe I will always love you my pumpkin George. You're the best lover any woman could ask for. Good bye."

She threw an air kiss his way.

"I'll see you in eternity my love."

~

I heard you. 'My pumpkin George'. Get a grip. I was married to him. He wasn't all that. Okay so he cheated on me. But he didn't leave me. He must have loved me. Don't call him that anymore. He was mine forever. He's in a grave right next to mine.

Oh my, that is scary. I don't want to be buried. Somebody help me. There's a lineup here of idiots that feel like they are paying their penance by giving me their true confessions. But it just makes me realize how little I knew my husband. We lived together as a couple for over forty years and I didn't know him at all. What a mystery.

Okay George, why didn't you leave me? I thought you loved me. Or did you? Maybe I was a convenience. You didn't like change. You like everything to stay the same.

Pat began to cry. Saliva began clogging the tube she was still holding in her mouth.

Oh damn! I can't breathe now. Look what you've done Laurie. Don't come here and taunt me. This is too much to handle. He was a jerk, but he was my husband, my George, not your 'Pumpkin' Grow up.

~

Laurie walked over to Pat's casket and said, "At least you have nice weather. Again I just want to say I'm sorry. Good bye."

~

As Laurie left, Pat cried hard and filled the tube with saliva. She couldn't seem to stop.

Nice weather huh?

Gurgle...blllop!

Suddenly; *Air...ohhh...Uhhh...uhhh...uhhh! I can't breathe... I can't breathe!*

The air tube was getting more and more difficult to breathe through, due to the position it had settled in, in the corner of Pat's mouth. She attempted to move her lips. Her tongue was able to move.

Blllop...

God... Thank you. I'm glad Frank put this tube in here. But... It's getting clogged up with something... Oh... My spit, I guess, or my tears. I have to stop crying. Now my mouth is getting so dry.

Just when Pat was giving up hope she heard a familiar voice.

~

"Pat, I'm here again."

~

Wanda. I'm so glad you're here!

~

"Hello My friend."

Wanda makes the sign of the cross. Nancy has joined Wanda but she stayed back not wanting to get dirt on her shoes.

"Nancy's here too. She just doesn't want to get her shoes dirty."

"Are you talking to Pat again? You're missing a link my dear. She's not here anymore. She's somewhere over the rainbow."

~

Yes, you are my friend, and that sounds like Nancy. Nancy or Wanda help me. Now get me outta here.

It's getting hard to breathe. I'm being entertained; I am listening to my husband's lovers. It's like listening to Soap Operas; more than one! It's getting hard to keep track. My man whore husband caused all this commotion. He sure was busy doing something. I heard it straight from the horse's mouth; or should I say horses' mouths; or even whores' mouths? Now I know how a priest feels. They are talking to me like they are in a confessional. In some ways it was cathartic. It kind of feels refreshing to hear truths from several so called friends.

I might as well take a jab at you and Nancy for not inviting me to that breakfast thing. Hey you two. I just want to say I know about the brunch, but the lies... You two are in deep. Telling a bunch of lies about me and my family, Mark told me everything. Everything you said to him came back to me.

So you're both blabber mouths. I just realized something. I forgave you and Nancy, both, for not inviting me to that breakfast that day the gossip started about me. You all must have had a great time. But I'm over it now.

Just get me out of here!

By the way, is that all you two have to do is spread dirty rumors about me? Hmm? and what do you think happened when I was eighteen? You both had no right gossiping to Mark your lies... Or, your version of the truth.

He went to your house to fix your plumbing, right? When he went over to work on your plumbing, your toilet I suppose, You gave him a dose of potty mouth right then and there! You told him, my nephew is really my son. Well, that is correct.

You and Nancy said you believed the father was Bill Shepherd.

You were once my good friend, Wanda, why did you have to spread that lie to Nancy. You were wrong! It wasn't Bills! I broke off several months before I got pregnant. I was in love with George. It was George's baby. We were young and in love. George never found out I was even pregnant. We were married four years later.

Bo came to my house once a week for years and George and I loved him as if he was our own child. But, he was officially adopted by my brother. My parents did the right thing for their grandson. He stayed in the family as a wonderful nephew. I know I should have told George; but I didn't. And now he's gone and if you don't get me out of here, I'll be joining him.

So there you have it dear Nancy and Wanda. Now do the right thing and help me out of this damn predicament. I'll tell you anything you want to know.

~

"You've been placed over the hole. I wonder if they are finally going to bury you soon," Wanda said shaking her head.

"Splat!" Wanda threw one glob of dirt on top of the casket as she had seen done in a movie. Feeling foolish she said, "I'm sorry I threw dirt again."

~

Wanda! Don't throw anymore dirt, please. You're like a child sometimes. Carol does that too. What's wrong with you girls?

~

Wanda threw dirt one more time on the casket. "Why haven't they buried you? I'm going to speak to that damn Blain. It's all about money. You poor, poor dear. Their probably waiting for cheap grave diggers. Damn, damn, damn! I'm going over to the office. I'll find him."

"Hey girl!" She put her head close to the casket. "I liked those cute warm looking pajamas your granddaughter gave you for your birthday. They looked comfy.

"How's that air tube? If you're not dead at least you can breathe!" She laughed quietly. "I would love to open this darn casket just once more. Something just doesn't seem right. Maybe I can rescue you from being buried alive."

Nancy gave her a dirty look.

~

Do it! Open it! Right! Right! You are correct! You know Wanda, I am getting sick, dear. I'm not dead. You got it! Now hurry get someone to help. Do this for me Wanda. I'll forgive the gossip. I need your help though. Right now!

Pat forced her finger to tap.

Tap...tap...scratch...scratch! A loud scratch is made.

~

"Good God! What did I hear? What was that? Shoot, I must be hearing things." Wanda turned. "I can't be doing this. This is driving me crazy. It's like I'm hearing scratching from inside the darn casket. I shouldn't have taken that last 'happy pill'."

"Well... I got to go. Bye!" Wanda makes the sign of the cross and began walking away.

~

Wait! This is not a dead person, this is a real live person, and I'm your friend! I'm really alive! You're correct, you did hear something. It was me. I thought you said maybe you could rescue me from being buried alive. Sometimes you actually make sense.

Oh damn! Sorry. I'm now getting frustrated. No one is listening to me. I'm sure it's because you can't hear a word I'm thinking. I tried to talk, nothing will come out.
Blllb...blllb...blllb...

~

"I'll check on you tomorrow."

~

"No! Wanda, come back! Waaa... No! Please come back. I'm not dead!

Her finger makes a slight tap.

~

Wanda turned and looked at the grave one last time. "Sweetie, I know you can hear me. I'll make sure you are buried by morning. Damn that Blain!"

Wanda walked away.

~

Pffft...pffft...pffft... Please No! Don't go, I'm not dead! No! Don't let them bury me!

Nancy Davis fast walked back to the casket at the cemetery. She already had walked two miles and she was determined to walk two more.

She first stopped at George's grave to place a fake yellow rose and throw an air kiss to it. She walked over to Pat's casket that was over the grave hole but still on the trolley.

"When are they going to bury you Pat?"

~

Nancy, it's you my friend. Well, have you come to save me Nancy? Thank God for you! I was just thinking about you.

I'm not sure if that rumor about you kissing George is true or not. I don't really believe it... You're too good of a friend.

Hey girl, I just realized you are probably the only person I can trust in the world. Well, besides Wanda.

~

"Pat, I'm here because I love you. You know that. I feel weird saying this. But... I have something that's been

on my mind for six years. That's a long time to hold
something in."

~

*Nancy, tell me good or bad, there is nothing that you
can say... Nothing... I mean that will change the deep
respect I have for you. You wouldn't believe all the true
confessions I've heard about my husband in the past
twenty-four hours. It's ridiculous!*

*I already know about the gossip that was spread about
my son Bo. You know now that the father is George. So
the cat's out of the bag.*

*You will always be my true friend. I remember when
you came by so often when I was sick in bed. You fed me,
bathed me, and you even did things for my family. You
took George shopping. You were nice enough to feed my
husband. You even made some of his favorite desserts.
Who does that?*

*You treated me like a sister. I really meant to thank
you, but I didn't and I'm so sorry. So for what it's worth,
thank you from the bottom of my heart.*

~

"Pat, remember when you were sick and I brought over a chicken casserole? Well remember you didn't have an appetite? I guess because you were feeling so very sick. Your temperature went sky high. Remember when George and I took you to the hospital because we couldn't get your fever down? Well it was then that I had an affair with George. Not ever in your bed. I would never do that. We did it in the room your granddaughter used when she stayed overnight. Well actually we did it on your sofa, and in your shower and I think we did it on your outside chaise lounge. I think we broke it. Oh my, I know we broke it when I fell off." She laughed. "But mostly we did the naughty at my house. So... No worries dear. We never ever would do it in your bed dear friend."

~

George, have all your tarts lined up at my casket? What? Nancy! Dear friend my ass. Did the naughty??? Huh? You mean screwed. You have to be pulling my leg. George would never do that to me. You must be making this up. You were my one true friend... I thought.

I'm feeling dizzy now. Dear God. This is like a nightmare, and I'm in it.

Diane told me about you. I thought she must be losing her mind. She saw you and George of all places at the parking lot of the church. When she said that, I almost dismissed it. But now all the tarts are claiming to be lost without you, George.

Did everybody have an affair with you? This can't be happening. George, it seems you were a very busy man. You weren't a man. I mean a very busy asshole that surely had a penis. But a man, nah! What I always thought you were was obviously a lie.

~

"Pat, remember when George said he was taking off to go on a fishing trip? Well... That trip was an experience I will never, ever forget. We went to Cancun and it was the most fun I have ever had in my entire life. George was not the stuffed shirt we all thought he was. In fact he was the opposite. He can be so sexy and fun. We went paragliding, we learned to scuba dive, we went exploring and even went skinny dipping, which was a first for me. He taught me how to fish. He never keeps them, the fish that is. He throws them back.

"What a man! You were so lucky to be married to such a wonderful man. God bless George. I sure can see what you saw in him. I know you missed him when he died Pat. Talking to you made me feel closer to you, because I was so heartbroken too.

"I missed him so much and I still do. We were like sisters then, remember? I'll bet you wondered how he came home so tan the week after his birthday. He told you he went fishing. We went to Cancun. Well, we did the naughty outside on our veranda, many times.

"Wow! I'm mesmerized at his stamina. He can be exhaustive. He didn't want to leave you though; you were the mother of his daughter. And he said he could never do that. I think he was too good to do that. You married the best man I ever knew. He will remain in my heart forever.

"So now you know why I have always wanted the best for you. George loved it when I did things for you. Because George would be so proud of me for helping take care of you. I put flowers on his grave every Sunday. I never missed."

~

So that's where those cheap plastic flowers came from. I visited George once a year on his birthday; that's once a year too many. I don't know which one of you was more conniving, you or George. He led me to believe I was the only woman in the world for him. And to think he went skinny dipping with my friend.

Damn you both. I had no reason to doubt him.

I'll bet you didn't know about the others. I'm sure he lied to you too. They all thought they were the only one.

He really went too far. I would have loved to have given him a haranguing. To show him what he's done to me. Just for five minutes, just one time.

I was a fool! I never saw any of it. How can I go on? Dear God, I'm crying. I feel tears rolling down my cheeks. I feel sick now. I'm losing air. And I don't care. If I don't get out of here, if I actually do die, I'll find you George. Even if I have to turn Hell inside-out! You'll be the first person I look for on your way down. You dirty rat!

How could you George?

~

"Pat, I need to say this: I want to be buried on the other side of George. He would have approved if he could. There is an empty plot there. That would be so perfect. I am still so much in love with him. It wasn't planned, but we were meant for each other. I wanted to clear it with you first."

~

Clear it with me? His wife? What do you think? You, want to be buried next to George, my husband? You definitely were meant for each other. The two people that I trusted the most in the world.

How could you Nancy? Why? What? Are you kidding me? I'm already feeling creepy vibes from you. Go home! Go find some loser at a bar at midnight and take him home. You can meet an animal there.

George was an asshole to lay down with you while I was in the hospital, now that I think about it, but you; what were you thinking? You had sex with your special friend's husband, then you started a prayer group, preaching we all need to look at ourselves and rid our demons.

Demons? Your such a hypocrite. The more I think about you with my husband, the more I now understand what you're made of. Your own demons were just getting started. You wanted our prayer group to have a special theme. You had a theme: What have you done for your neighbor lately? Wanda and I thought it was kind of strange. But how could you treat me, a neighbor, so cruelly?

Now I realize what you were up to. You wanted forgiveness for what you were doing to me, your friend and neighbor. For the sake of your friends. This was a kick in the pants to all your friends. What you did for your neighbor was unthinkable? Wow! I guess you felt you were doing good for me?

You could get your fix anywhere. Why my husband, your once upon a time friend? Why? Leave your friend's husbands alone.

Oh, I forgot, you don't know the meaning of friends. That's so wrong. It was unforgiveable Nancy. Remember just a few minutes ago I said there is nothing you could say that would change the deep respect that I had for you? Well I lied. That takes the cake. That changes everything girl.

If I am lucky enough to get out of here, you better hope we don't pass each other by on the street. You now disgust me. What you did will never be forgiven.

Oh wait... Get me outta here and I may reconsider.

~

"Pat, I just realized something, I love you, my sweet friend."

~

Nancy... Shut your pie hole!

~

"Wanda... How long have you been standing there?"

"Not long Nancy. But I guess long enough. I thought you told me you weren't coming back to the cemetery today."

"I guess I changed my mind at the last minute. But I'm headed home now. Why are you here?"

"I do walk to the cemetery without you sometimes."

"I just had a private chat with Pat."

"Okay... Goodbye Nancy." Wanda began to leave.

Nancy stopped her and said, "I would like to talk to someone in charge also. How do I get in touch with that Blain guy?"

~

Wanda, don't trust that woman. She's a wolf in sheep's clothing. She will never be in charge of my care. She is nothing to me. Nothing!

That anger made me use all my energy. I'm feeling weak now. Thanks a lot Nancy; now I'm weak and exhausted.

George, how could you?

~

"I walked over to the office looking for Blain myself. I couldn't find him anywhere. I must have walked five miles today and now I'm getting tired. I left Blain a note with my phone number on it."

"Well I'll just go home then, Wanda. Want to walk in the morning friend?"

~

Don't listen to her Wanda. She just called you friend. She doesn't even know what that word means. She doesn't like you. You're just a pawn to her.

~

"Maybe, if I get up at the crack of dawn. But I'm pretty tired."

"Well I'll meet you at eight a.m. at the cemetery entrance if you want."

"Okay. Bye."

~

Don't let the ghosts bite you on your ass Nancy! Here's your hat what's your hurry? Good riddance! Ignoramus!

~

"Well... Here we are Pat. I tried, but Blain is playing 'missing in action'. I did try. At least you had your good friend Nancy to listen to for a while.

"Were you listening to Nancy?"

~

Oh you have no clue. Sure, friend, you have no idea what just came out of her mouth. I listened alright. If you only knew. Hmm... Maybe you do know. I wonder. I believe I can trust you, but I'm not sure of anything now. Did you know about my husband and Nancy? That's a good question that may never be answered. How long were you standing there Wanda?

~

"I heard everything, you poor girl.

"Pat, I want you to know Nancy had that breakfast brunch and invited friends I didn't even know. But she specifically said, 'We are not inviting Pat. She is the enemy. The enemy!' I didn't know why she said that. She didn't think you treated George well when he was alive.

She thought you worked him to death and that's why he died.

"I told her I didn't believe her. I thought he might be having an affair with someone but God only knows who. She disagreed. She said he would never cheat on you. But I guess I believed differently. And I was right!

George was away from you so much, I thought something was up. I guess I'm too much of a busy body but, I meant well Pat. I care about you and wish things had turned out differently.

"I sure miss you."

~

*Wanda, your intuition is spot on. You **are** my friend. You hit the nail on the head. I'm sorry about mistrusting you. You are a blessing.*

Now, we're not going to worry about Nancy. She is over to me. Carol is actually becoming a surprise to me. But Nancy is nothing but a 'Devil made her do it' trouble maker.

Let's just get me out of here. I'm in a stupid situation. Wanda, I am not dead. Please, please, please get me out of here.

I'm starting to feel weak. My breathing is getting harder. I'm feeling dizzy. I really need your help. Please don't disappoint me Wanda.

~

"I wonder why you don't reek yet. I thought since you weren't embalmed you should be getting kind of stinky. It still smells like flowers and just the outdoors. I'm beginning to feel kind of skeptical more and more. This is not normal. I wonder where Mark is. I haven't seen him since your funeral.

"Well, maybe the casket is just sealed too well to smell you."

~

I don't stink! You know the stench of a dead body? Good. Now that's a clue Wanda. You are so smart. You are answering your own question. How can she be dead and not smell? They bathed me with Lysol in the funeral home. I should smell like a hospital. Well you answered the million dollar question. You can't unless... What? Come on Wanda, I know you... Because I'm not dead!

~

"I keep saying it, because something doesn't feel right. Well I'm leaving Pat. Take care. It's going to be a cool evening. I hope that will be a good night for you. I'll be back soon. Bye girlfriend."

~

Wanda, don't go girlfriend. Oh no! I don't know how much longer I can hold out. I'm feeling pretty sick now. Please don't go Wanda. I want to scream about the recent confessions I've heard.

Kitten was a shocker. One big surprise was from Laurie Shepherd, from my book club. I would have never guessed that one. But Nancy, my once a upon a time best friend; it's hard to comprehend.

Wanda please stay. I need to talk to someone. And I do believe you and Carol are the only two friends I can trust.

Nancy sure knows how to ruin a person's day.

I am getting sleepy.

Wanda later stopped at the local Rocky's Supermarket where she bumped into Mark.

"Hi, I just stopped at the cemetery and they haven't buried Pat yet."

Mark looked annoyed by the news. His eyes were red.

"Are you okay?" Wanda patted his shoulder. "Do you need a tissue?" Wanda handed Mark a tissue.

"Oh, sure. I have these allergies, and they won't go away." Mark blew his nose. He sneezed twice and laughed. "I'm a mess."

"I have just the thing." Wanda looked in her pocket book.

"No, no. I have been on a generic allergy medicine and it'll get better soon. Well, I'm late for a doctor appointment, see ya later!"

He was obviously taking Pat's death harder than anyone thought.

Wanda arrived home rubbing her temples in a circular motion. The phone was ringing off the hook.

"Who could that be?" Wanda picked up the phone.

"Hi! ... Carol? ... No! And someone is going to answer to this. It's illegal. She wasn't embalmed Carol. He could lose his license. Damn him. But do you want to know a strange thing I noticed. There is no odor. What do you make of that?"

Carol agreed that was strange. And she agreed with Wanda about all the strange sounds she heard during the funeral. "I know of a good attorney."

"What would that accomplish?"

Carol said, "If they don't put her in the ground the cemetery, Blain I mean, could be sued."

"The family is probably already looking into that by now. But the fact that she doesn't have a stench is strange. Well, maybe the coffin is just sealed too well to notice."

Larry called Michelle asking one last time if she would go to the prom with him. He felt pretty desperate. He apologized for being a jerk and he didn't mean to cause trouble with Michael. He was just over the top jealous.

"It's in a few hours. What... Are you going to get a tux... Like *now*? Don't be silly. Michael and I have a thing going now and I want to keep it that way. *We* can't be anything anymore Larry. It's over."

Michelle said she felt bad. "Larry, I just don't think our relationship was going anywhere."

She reminded him about his goofy friends, Brian and Scott, who met up with Michael after school and tormented him. He didn't fight back when Scott pushed him at the basketball court. Michael just walked away.

"He's my kind of friend Larry. He chose not to fight back."

Larry slammed the phone down and decided he wasn't going to go to the prom without Michelle. But, he wasn't through with Michael and Michelle yet. He ripped up his ticket.

They'll pay! he thought.

Scott and Brian were there with him. They weren't going to the prom either.

He said to them, "Let's go do something that might wake a couple people up."

Brian's brother Greg was joining them. He was a couple years younger but wanted to feel cool, so he decided to join his brother for the evening.

Larry said, "We are just getting started."

Scott laughed. "Does your idea include beer?"

Larry shook his head. "No, not this time. Well who knows maybe... But I have to see if I can get a rise from Michael or Michelle first. She already hates me. She'll be sorry."

That evening was cool; not freezing, but chilly, and the temperature was expected to drop ten degrees.

At May's house Michelle was dressed in her beautiful purple gown that was homemade by her grandmother, Pat. She was excited and sad at the same time. Pictures were going to be taken at the park's boat dock and Pat had planned to be present.

May and Bo drove the couple to the park and Dan and Frank joined them and took several pictures of the well dressed couple in various poses.

Bo met them and took several pictures himself. Bo gave Michelle and Michael the keys to his dark grey Mercedes for the evening.

"I trust you Michelle." She couldn't be happier.

They all waved good bye to the couple and watched as Michael had no trouble navigating the luxury car.

Bo hugged May and said, "Your daughter is beautiful."

They were headed to the Hilton for the dinner and festivities. May and Dan kissed Michelle and the couple left.

Bo and May both hugged for an extra long time, then May burst out crying, "Mommy you missed it. Beautiful Michelle in the gown you made her."

The handsome couple left. The rest went back to May and Dan's house.

Pat was beginning to feel a chill. She was afraid that it was inevitable she would be downright cold soon. She tried hard to move her body but it wouldn't move.

Why am I so cold? Why don't they put heaters in these things? Okay Pat don't be silly. Just turn your thoughts to something that pleases you.

Michelle, this is your prom night. I wish I would have had the chance to see you, but I'm sure you're at your prom by now. It must be evening... Or is it? It's cold enough to be evening.

I remember when you tried your gown on. How beautiful you looked. I can only imagine what you looked like tonight. By now, my little princess, you're headed to the prom.

I'm feeling mighty cold now. I wonder how long I'll last if it drops down to freezing.

All of a sudden she felt like she was moving.

What... What's going on? Is someone moving me? Where am I? I feel like I'm being moved in my casket. I hear voices. It sounds like young kids. Who are they? Help! They can't hear me.

~

"Brian, she's heavy. We have to lift up and in."

Larry, Brian, Scott and Greg were all attempting to put Pat's casket up in the bed of an old Ford pickup truck. They had backed the truck, with the tailgate down, over the grave, straddling it, until it was nearly touching the casket sitting on the casket trolley. Now the casket was a bit below the tailgate and had to be manhandled up into the truck bed.

Scott knew how to take the casket off the trolley because he had had a part time job working with the diggers at the cemetery. But he was a weakling and he couldn't quite get the casket high enough onto the truck.

They all kept trying until finally Larry had an idea. He definitely didn't want to mess his older brother Bob's truck in any way or he would never be allowed to use it again. He didn't want to wake the dead either. It felt pretty eerie being in a cemetery at dusk. Also he knew Mrs. Faros and didn't want anything to happen to her.

"Be careful," Larry said, "I don't want to harm Nan in any way... I mean Mrs. Faros. She's my friend. She's always been good to me."

~

Is that you Larry? I'm not your Nan! Well friend, maybe if you get me outta here. Where are you taking me? Just rescue me Larry for goodness sakes.

~

There was an army blanket in the bed of the truck. The truck was higher than the casket on the trolley, so the boys lifted one end and leaned it causing the casket to be on its end. They maneuvered the blanket under the casket to reduce friction. They tried to push it deep into the bed of the truck. To their consternation, the truck's toolbox was located parallel to the bed, rather than across it as is usual. This stopped the casket. They had to tilt the casket on its side, almost completely, and rest it on the toolbox. That worked perfectly.

Now they had the casket. They quickly took off across the grass and down the bumpy path to the highway. It was dusk and they were hoping no one saw them.

"Where are we going?" Greg asked. He was only sixteen and knew what he was doing was not good. He was showing obvious signs of fear. "This is too weird. I don't want to be a part of this."

~

Who are you guys? You almost turned me upside down. But one thing is for sure... I feel pain. I bumped my head and it hurts. I felt that, and I'm cold and my charley horse is back.

I'm without question alive and scared half to death.

If that's you Larry you're not helping me now. What in the heavens above are you doing? You're going to be in big trouble buster.

I think I can talk. Help! Maybe somebody is trying to save me. Help! I'm alive, I'm alive. Maybe Larry is trying to save me. No way, he's probably doing something mischievous and against the law. He probably thinks I'm some zombie or something. But what does he want with my body? He wouldn't. Oh my God, not that!

Owww, that hurt. I'm being driven somewhere. It's a bumpy ride. But I'm still in my casket. Where are you taking me? This is great... I think. It's nighttime... I think... Isn't it? I shouldn't be going anywhere if I'm in a casket and its night time. I should stay put in my grave, shouldn't I?

This is weird. Something is wrong. Body snatchers? I'm being body snatched. Maybe they won't bury me. Good. I could call for help.

Help! This is a bouncy ride. It's starting to hurt me. No one can hear me, who am I kidding.

But where are you taking me Larry?

~

Brian said, "Larry we better not get caught, my little brother's with me."

Greg said, "I'm kind of scared. I want to go home. The cops are always at the park."

Larry shushed him, "Shhh... We're only taking her to Michael's back yard."

They pulled up to a two story brick home in a nice neighborhood. The front light was on but everything else was dark. So they had to be extremely careful. As they pulled up and stopped beyond the driveway they saw a lit cigarette shining on the front porch.

Larry said, "That must be his father. He's looking at us. We're dead! Don't stop! Keep going!"

Brian cried, "I'm out!"

Greg whined, "Me too! I'm on the honor roll. You guys are going to get me in a lot of trouble. I wish I never came with you guys."

Greg asked, "Do you think he can tell it's a casket in the back of the truck?"

Larry confidently said, "Oh no way. But we can't leave the body on the driveway. He might be sitting out there for a long time. Change of plans!"

Suddenly a Mercedes pulled up and Larry could see Michael dressed in his tux get out of the car and open the passenger door for Michelle. She got out of the car and Michael's father and mother took pictures of the couple with a flash camera by a beautiful flowering shrub. Larry parked in front, hoping not to be seen. He became a bit nervous, but he wanted to watch.

Larry said, "I got it. Let's take the body to the prom, and leave it in the parking lot."

Brian and Greg replied, "No, I'm not getting involved in that."

Scott laughed. "Yeah, I'm in. That'll shock him."

Larry drove down the road to an intersection near Brian's house.

"See you guys." Brian and Greg jumped out of the truck and ran down their street, hoping not to be seen. "You guys are nuts. See ya!"

Larry shook his head. "I think I've got it. Where will they go after the prom?"

Scott said, "Maybe their house."

"No, Scott, they'll get some beer and go to the park."

Scott said, "I've got it. Since we're driving down this road anyway, let's go to the park and put the casket on our picnic table. The one down near the dock. You know, the one by the lake is perfect. We could look inside! I have a flashlight. Brian and Greg are going to miss out on this."

"Who cares? I just want to see their faces when they see the casket."

Larry looked shocked. "Are we crazy? Are we going to stay here all night waiting for them? I might be looking at twenty years in prison."

Scott laughed. "No way man. No you won't... Probably only fifteen."

"Well, I won't be able to graduate. Worse than anything, Michelle will never speak to me again. Well, maybe that's not so bad. She ruined my prom night. She probably hates me anyway."

~

Pat was bouncing around in the casket. She was luckily able to catch the whistle somehow in her hand that was lying open, palm up.

Pat, I'm so proud of you! You've got this.

In her excitement, she let the whistle slide down next to her hand.

Come on Pat, You can do it.

Humph...pfft.

She tried to move her hand, but it wouldn't budge. Her pointer finger was alive though. She pushed and the whistle moved. It was a struggle but she persevered.

One more time.

She extended her finger and felt the whistle. It was so close, but she couldn't get it up to her mouth.

Wanda had not been hospitable to Carol the day they met at the cemetery. Mostly, she ignored her, and she'd left with a sense of overwhelming guilt. She worked out an excuse to contact her and make things right. A dinner date, that might work at patching things up.

Wanda called Carol early enough for dinner. Carol answered the call from Wanda.

"Hi! it's me."

"Hi Carol."

"Have you eaten dinner?"

"Ah... No. Not yet."

"I'm calling to see if you want to go out for a bite? We can go for a Saturday night special dinner at the Toodle House."

"Well it's not so early, its six thirty and its prom night we might run into a barrage of teenagers."

They both laugh.

Wanda smirked. "They probably wouldn't be at the Toodle House. They'd go to the Hilton and buy steak or lobster. After all it's on mom and pop's tab." They both laughed again.

"Sure I would like that very much."

The Toodle House was everyone's favorite family restaurant in Chalfont. The food was country-home good and they both knew the owner, Katy Ann Parker. She did all the cooking, with all homemade desserts. The best dessert was the chocolate dump cake. It was so good. Sometimes folks would just stop by for dessert.

Without pausing for a response, Wanda started right in on her apology. "I'm sorry I didn't help you up yesterday when you fell at the cemetery. I did see you when you fell. I was on another planet thinking about that poor girl in her coffin. So quick she passed and so, so sad."

Carol listened half heartedly to the weak apology. Wanda's call was confusing but she did feel happy that Wanda called at all.

She was getting around quite well on her injured leg that had happened a couple weeks ago. They thought it would take months to heal. Although her knee does need therapy, she continued to get around quite well under the circumstances.

When she fell at the cemetery none of her friends offered to help. Anyone besides the grounds keeper could have come to her rescue at the cemetery.

She's suddenly over it. "I'm exhausted from my long walk today. I had to bathe Finnegan. He was so sweet. He looked like a new dog after his bath.

"I was taken aback when Finnegan pooped on George's grave though." They both chuckled. "He sure seemed to know Pat's grave site, with all that barking and making a scene! I swear, he knew she was there, somewhere."

Most of the girls disliked 'Chief Georgie'. They secretly named him when he was alive. He had been a Chief Petty Officer in the Navy and was bitter since he never advanced his rate to Senior Chief before he retired. He seemed to take it out on poor Pat. She simply paid no mind. He thought he was her Commander-in-chief, but she knew how to tackle whatever he threw at her.

"I think he was having an affair. I don't have any suspicions with whom, but he was off to somewhere, USA, all the time. Pat didn't seem to think so though... I don't think. She was madly in love with him. To her he could do no wrong. After what I've learned, though, I'm beginning to wonder."

They ended their chit-chat with a dinner date for that evening after Finnegan's walk.

Pat noticed her middle finger still had movement but she could not quite reach over the satin material and onto the coffin's wood. Her pointer finger's fingernail was sheared off and it was bleeding. She had lost part of the nail to the quick. It was so painful that she barely noticed the stickiness from the blood.

The bouncing of the truck caused her to move further away from the bell and the whistle. The tube was getting clogged with rain water and spit. She was quickly losing air, and she knew something had to give, and real soon.

These kids were up to no good she believed. At least they were prolonging the time she'd have on earth. They couldn't bury her if they don't have a body.

She said to herself, *It's now or never Pat.*

She strained to move her sore finger; only the middle finger was working now. It was cramping just like her foot. It was going into a spasm.

Oh dear God, I can hardly breath. And I can't reach the side of the casket?

What's going on Larry? I'm on my side, I think. Maybe my thumb can help. Help... Help! I need help.

Larry where are you?

I need water. Maybe I can get some from that tube. But where is it now? My weight pulled me over. What in the world? I must be lying on my right arm because I feel quite uncomfortable.

The truck had been driving on a bumpy dirt surface. It came to a sudden and painful stop for Pat.

The boys went around to the back of the truck and pushed the casket onto something with a loud and hurtful kerplop.

Owww!

Pat felt the casket being moved and her body bounced with a loud thump. She felt her body was now level again.

Ouch, that really hurt Larry. What did you just do?

The waxing gibbous moon was shining down, providing an eerie light that offered adequate visibility.

Larry and Scott had to push the casket onto the picnic table. They again used the army blanket that was lying flat on the floor of the truck bed as an aid to sliding the heavy casket.

Larry said, "I don't want to hurt her, I hope she's okay."

Scott laughed, "Larry, she's dead, man. I don't think she'll ever be okay again."

They had to slide the casket back off the toolbox, straighten it out, get it level on the truck bed, then slide it back carefully so it wouldn't fall off. Scott looked exhausted.

"Man that was rad. We did it, we almost moved a coffin off the truck and onto the picnic table and you didn't bang up your brother's truck."

Scott said, "We still have one more step. It's going to wake the dead when it drops off the back of the truck."

~

Pat heard someone say the words picnic table. Although she was frightened this was promising, she thought.

She noticed dampness on her cheeks and realized that she had started crying real tears again. She also realized that the body snatchers have begun lifting and pushing the casket onto, she believed, a picnic table somewhere.

She thought, *Where am I?*

She was feeling more alert at this point.

~

Larry pulled and Scott pushed until the casket slid completely off the truck and with a loud '**bang**', landed squarely onto the table.

~

The movement seemed to stop. But the jostling had caused her a bruise or two for sure.

~

Larry said aloud, "We did it!"
Scott meowed like a cat.

~

She was now at the hands of a gaggle of teenagers and she was their crazy whim.
Why are they laughing? They must be trying to get the lid of the casket open. Good, she thought.

~

Scott said, "Cool beans, I found a flash light. Let's see what she looks like."

Dusk had now turned into night. He flashed it onto the lid of the casket.

Larry looked inside the tool chest. "Voila!" He pulled out a hammer and screw driver. They poked with the screw driver. But it was like fort Knox. *This was not going to be easy,* they thought. It was so secure. Larry couldn't figure how to open it.

"I have a hammer. Maybe I can break the hinge."

Scott said, "That would be so rad."

Larry began probing and hammering. He pulled his wallet out of his back pocket and put it on the picnic table. He was afraid it would fall out onto the grass.

~

What in God's name are you doing to my casket Larry? That's got to be you. Open the latch, you ignoramus. Keep looking, it's on the right. You're probably on the left. Come on Larry. You definitely have a teenager's brain, probably so full of carbohydrates you're living in a fog. Now just open the damn thing.

~

"I think I can just open it," Larry told Scott. He had noticed the latches and was working them. He then lifted the lid of the casket.

"Shine the flash light on the body."

Both boys gaped at the sight. "Oh my Gosh! Look!"

Carol peered at her watch and grabbed her rain poncho as she listened to the weather man call for possible showers. The forecaster was saying, "It's going down to the low forties or possibly the thirties. It's going to be a chilly, rainy, spring evening, so bundle up."

Finnegan was whimpering and pacing back and forth in front of the door.

"Okay… Okay."

Carol opened the door and the dog sneakily slipped out and ran down the street. Without her cane, Carol rushed outside. She limped down the street frantically on a futile chase after him. She called, "Finnegan, please come home!"

Wanda saw the canine escape artist as she pulled up in front of Carol's house. She jumped out of her car after witnessing the disaster. She ran toward Finnegan's trail.

She called over to Carol, "I see him! I'll help. I've got this side of the street."

She stayed on the opposite side of the street. They fast walked in parallel with each other.

Finnegan was a step ahead of Wanda. She could see Carol was limping and struggling to run. She called him. "Finnegan! I bought you your favorite treats."

He didn't even slow down. He seemed to have an agenda. He darted across the street and a car barely missed him. Both women screamed.

"Finnegan, please come back. I'm so sorry you're not happy. Please come back dear Finney," Carol cried. "I love you Finney. Don't leave me now. I really care about you now."

Wanda whistled for Finnegan but he began running faster. He didn't slow down at all.

Carol shouted, "We forgot he's deaf!"

He was now running as fast as those little legs could go. He was like the flash and was out of sight in moments. But both Wanda and Carol knew where he was headed.

"Carol!" Wanda shrieked. "He looks like he is heading toward the cemetery. We should get in my car and follow him."

Carol dashed back to Wanda's car with a strong limp and jumped in. They headed in the direction of the cemetery.

The two women pulled up in front of Pat's gravesite. Wanda said excitedly, "The diggers must have been here. I don't see Pat's casket?"

Wanda and Carol jumped out of the car in unison. "Quick, here he comes," Carol cried. "Catch him!"

"Come on my baby," Carol called to the little speed demon. "Here Finney, come to mommy."

Wanda, exhausted from chasing the dog, said, "Where's the casket? Oh my God. It's gone. The hole is still there but the casket is gone. She wasn't buried. She's missing. Who would take a casket?"

Carol almost reached Finney, but he took off. He was on a roll.

"What in the world is going on here? Has everyone gone crazy?"

Carol called May on the phone.

"Hi Carol, what's up?"

"May, did you know the casket is not here?"

"What... Where are you?"

"I'm at the cemetery with Wanda."

"It's getting dark. Why are you at the cemetery at night?"

"Yes. Well Carol and I were trying to catch Finnegan. He ran to the cemetery. I caught up with him and low and behold, he looked for the casket too. It's just not here. He took off. Maybe he knows where she is. We're getting ready to leave. Wanda and I are going to look for Finnegan, but you better try and find out what happened to your poor mother."

"That's ridiculous. Who would take a casket with a body in it? Maybe it's that stupid Larry."

"Who?"

"No one... Thanks."

"Well I'm still looking for Finnegan, but maybe you could stop by here with the police. This is all too weird. They said they were getting ready to bury her in the morning. That was the last word I heard from Blain."

"Dan and I will be right there. Bye."

May had just taken her shower from a long day of grieving for her mother, and yet happiness for her daughter's prom night. She felt quite upset and this had suddenly caused her to want to call her mother. Then reality set in. She walked over to her husband who was falling asleep in his lounge chair.

"Dan, Mommy's casket's gone!"

Dan stared straight ahead. "What... With your mother in it? That's insane."

"Yes, yes. Get dressed please, and I'll call Uncle Frank."

"I can go in my sweats. I'm ready."

They jumped in Dan's truck and off to the cemetery they went. Frank had said he would meet them there.

When they pulled up to the cemetery they could see the media was already there.

May shook her head, "Oh great. Now what?"

Wanda had called Nancy on her cell phone and told her that Pat's casket was missing. Nancy hung up and immediately called the police and the newspaper.

Within an hour of discovering the missing casket, several police cars and newspaper reporters were already gathered at the cemetery plot. They discovered that the body had been snatched and the news TV crew announced that a family member, Frank Brigham, offered a five thousand dollar reward for leads to the missing body.

The whole family was called by Kathryn letting them know the sad circumstances. Many folks were attempting to help by searching for the missing casket. Finnegan was found running down Main Street heading toward the state park. Officer Bob collected the dog and kept him in his car while they searched for the casket.

Okay, okay. Stop shining that light on my face now.

Larry, I'm not mad at you. This was so wrong that it's right. I know in the past I've called you a 'ding bat'. I sometimes have had a forked tongue. You don't always think very straight, but you came through though.

All my family heard me tapping and scratching and nobody caught on. Nobody figured it out that something was wrong. Somebody had to save me even if it's a dummkopf like you.

Sorry again for calling you a name.

Maybe I can blink my eyes.

Humph...humph...humph.

I can see... I think. I see a glare. It's really bright. Could you tone it down a notch?

The flashlight was beginning to hurt Pat's eyes. Her finger tapped on the edge of the casket.

Tap tap...

~

"What was that?" Larry screeched, as he stared with a questioning gape at whoever was in the casket? *It's Nan. She looks too good*, he thought. *Is it Mrs. Faros? She doesn't look dead. What did I hear?*

"It kind of sounded like a tap tap. Wow. Cool beans! Maybe she's a zombie," Scott said, as he goggled at the woman in the casket with his mouth wide open.

Larry whispered to Scott, "She looks too much like she's alive. She looks like she could just walk out of this dang casket at any time. "

He saw the whistle and nervously laughed. "Maybe I'll try this thing."

He put it into Pat's closed lips. "There you go. Now if you are a walking dead you must blow that whistle." They both giggle with a bit of cautious fear.

~

I can blow the whistle, I think. I am definitely a walking dead person... Pfff...pffft...

Wheyooo. The whistle was loud and clear.

I did it. Thank you, God. I knew they would find me. I can breathe now. I can see, Even though it's black as night. But I'm alive and now they will find me. Won't they Larry?

Larry, where are you?

~

"Damn!" Larry goggled in shock as he noticed Pats pursed lips around the whistle. They watched as Pat's eyes blinked. When the whistle blew, they screamed, "Help! She must be the living-dead! Oh my Gosh! Scott, we gotta get outta here."

Larry jumped up and he and Scott screamed, "Help!"

"Larry!" Pat croaked painfully. "It's me... Pat... Mrs. Faros... You know, Michelle's grandmom."

The boys stared in shock, then they jumped into the truck as fast as they could go and drove off.

Strange. Where did you go?

Now that's just great. He's afraid of me. He saved me and now he takes off. Again... You never cease to amaze me Larry.

"Come back! I won't haunt you."

Pat blew the whistle non-stop.

Well at least I can breathe. Now that I have air maybe I can scream.

She tried to scream, but was only able to choke out the word, "Help!" over and over.

Larry and Scott drove away for a moment not speaking a word to each other. Then out of nowhere. "Oh my God. I think I heard her say my name."

They had left the casket open. To make it a double whammy they had forgot Larry's wallet on the picnic table.

Then they saw police cars speeding toward the park.

"I didn't close the casket!" Larry screamed. "And I left my wallet on the picnic table. We're in deep. We're dead Scott. It's supposed to rain tonight. She'll find us. Now we're doomed!"

Their eyes were as wide as saucers.

One of the cop cars made a U-turn at the entrance to the park and began chasing Larry's truck. He was clocked at twenty miles over the speed limit. They stopped him on a speeding violation. The cop was Officer Bob, an old friend of Pat's.

"Where are you boys going in such a hurry?"

"Home officer," Larry said with fright still on his face.

While they are parked on the side of the road, a distant whistle could be heard.

Larry said, "Don't go in there officer. The park that is. The body is dead but that woman is now living. She's a walking dead. I don't know if she walks. She's a whistle blowing dead. That whistle you hear, that's her. The walking dead can do almost anything. If you get them mad, you're doomed. Did you hear it officer? She's whistling again. She called my name, Larry. She knows it was me that moved her. She'll be after me. Don't let her get us."

Scott looked excited and said, "Cool man!"

"What in the world are you babbling about? License and registration young man."

Larry looked for his wallet. "Oh no, it's not in my pocket. I think I left it on the picnic table in the park. Next to her. It's right where she is. Officer, please, don't let her get me."

Officer Bob said, "Very well... Let's go get your license before it's lost forever. I won't let anyone get you. Why aren't you boys at the prom?"

"We are the ones that moved the body officer. We didn't mean anything by it. They never buried Mrs. Faros anyway... She was just lying there in her casket."

Scott slumped down in the seat. "I just came along for the ride, man."

Suddenly, Finnegan jumped out of the police car and ran through the park entrance.

Officer Bob opened the back door of his car and told the boys to jump in. He spoke on his radio, "Body of Patricia Faros in park in casket on picnic table. On my way. Two boys are in custody. In pursuit of the poodle dog, he's running in the park."

"We didn't want to go to the prom for personal reasons Officer Bob." Scott just shook his head and meowed like a cat.

Officer Bob looked back at Scott. "What's wrong with you young man?"

Scott laughed. "Nothing officer, I'm just pumped up man."

"Where is the body? We're going to find it and you two appear to be in big trouble. What were you thinking? That's a criminal offense."

"Straight down toward the lake where the picnic tables are located, You're heading the right way. Follow Finnegan," Larry said.

Finnegan's little legs were running as fast as they could go. The police car was in chase.

"Why did you move the casket down here to the park?"

"Well... It's a long story. But it's because I wanted to get my girlfriend's attention. That's her grandmother. I had no idea she would be a zombie. She opened her eyes when we opened the casket. She blew the whistle I gave her for her birthday. Man...We ran as fast as we could go, that's why I forgot my wallet with my license in it, and that's why I was driving so fast. Man! I wanted to get outta there. I never saw a dead person, let alone a living-dead person."

Scott grinned and said, "She looked so rad, man. She was really mad at Larry."

"I'll be taking you boys downtown for booking after this. You have no idea how much trouble you're in. What were you thinking? You know you might have to do some time."

Scott sat back and said, "Cool! I'm in a cop car on a chase. This is so rad. Wait till I tell my mom."

"How did you boys get the casket in your truck?"

Scott said, "Whoa, it was heavy man. But we are stronger than the hulk. We did it with brute force man!"

"Yes, sir. We were able to slide it in. But... I'm afraid to tell you... The body is alive... I swear! Please don't go in there. You'll be sorry. I'm afraid to go anywhere near there."

Scott shook his head and said, "That body's the living-dead, man. She'll kill us. She's blowing the whistle Larry put in the casket. I don't think she's too happy with us."

Officer Bob said, "If you hurt one hair on that woman's dead body, you two will be seeing four walls for a very long, long time."

Scott replied, "We didn't hurt her Officer Bob. She's really cool. I think we helped her. She wants to live again. That's all."

Larry whined, "She called my name. Oh God. That means she knows it was me that snatched her body. She'll be after me!"

"You're saying she talked to you?"

Scott said, "Yep... She said, *'Laaarrryyy'*. I'm glad she didn't know who I was, or say *my* name. I lucked out."

Finnegan led the police car and ran into the park, straight to the picnic table.

Officer Bob told the boys to stay back. He saw the dog jump up on the picnic table and into the casket.

"Oh my God. I don't believe what I just saw."

He beamed his flashlight into the casket and low and behold, Pat was crying and kissing Finnegan. She was saying in a hoarse whisper, "My hero dog... You found me!"

Officer Bob said, "Pat is that you?"

"Yes... Oh my God! Bob, it is me... Yes! I'm alive... I'm alive! Thank God, I'm alive. I'm saved. It is me, and my dog found me. How lucky is that?" She said aloud, in an increasingly stronger voice. "Officer Bob, will you thank Larry and his crazy friend for saving me. Oh, and by the way, I'm freezing. Do you have a blanket?"

The police officer stood over Pat smiling from ear to ear. He looked back at his car and said, "No one is going to believe this story. I can barely believe it myself."

He reached over and picked up the wallet that was behind the casket. He then went to his car, handed Larry his wallet and briefed the other officers by radio on the findings. Following an excited conversation with the other officers, he then grabbed a blanket out of the trunk. He walked over to Pat who was being kissed by a happy dog. Officer Bob carefully covered Pat with the warm blanket. An ambulance was heard in the distance.

"They're on their way Pat. You're safe and you're saved."

"Oh my God, thank you. Thank you Larry and that other guy, and thank you Finnegan my sweet dog. What would I do without you?

"Going home Finnegan. I hear the ambulance. You have no idea how wonderful it feels. I can't tell you how happy I am. You saved my life. Where is Larry?"

Officer Bob said, "We're going to take him down to the station for questioning."

"Can I speak with him for just a moment." Pat began to have some difficulty speaking. She stuttered some of the words. She attempted to speak but it took a minute. "He sa...sa...saved my li...life."

Bob said, "I guess you're right. Let me get him for you."

Officer Bob opened the back door shaking his head. He said, "I'm not through with you boys yet, but Pat would like to speak with both of you."

Larry looked at Scott, "Is it safe? You know she was dead?"

Officer Bob looked at the boys, losing his patience, and said, "Go over to the casket right now and talk to Mrs. Faros. She's alive. She's not some zombie. You actually saved her life."

Larry said, "Well she won't hurt me will she?"

"No, of course not. She's alive. She'll thank you. She's not dead. You saved her life."

Officer Bob gawked at Scott when he said, "Cool man."

The boys walked over to Pat and they both looked at her with caution. Larry said, "Hi Mrs. Faros. How's it going? You sure don't look dead."

Pat smiled at Larry and said, "Well I'm not dead Larry because of you two. If it wasn't for you and who ever that other guy was..."

Larry said, "His name is Scott."

"Yes, Scott. If it wasn't for you two, I would be heading for my burial soon... I guess in the morning. You two saved my life. You have no idea what this means to me. I can't thank you enough.

"How did you two know I was alive?"

Larry said, "I just had a funny feeling something was just not right. I was curious about the whole thing."

Scott said, "I just thought it would be cool to see a dead person. I just wanted to see what you looked like."

"Thank you my friends. I will always be grateful to you two for saving my life."

Scott said, "Cool man. We thought you were a dead person. We saved someone's life. My mom's not going to believe this."

Scott asked the officer with confusion "Does this mean we're heroes?"

"Yes, that's exactly what that means. However, you did break the law. I'm sure you won't be going to jail. But maybe community service like cleaning up the park will suffice."

The ambulance pulled up and the paramedics jumped out and gathered Pat onto the stretcher. She threw a kiss to the boys and asked if Finnegan would be allowed to be brought to the hospital with her. Unfortunately the emergency crew said no. Until they left Finnegan could stay at pat's feet.

Finnegan cuddled into Pat's neck, ignoring the crew's directions,

Pat kissed Finnegan, and with her right arm she was able to hold him the way she did every night while they watched animal planet together. Finnegan lapped at her face all over and kissed her frantically. He knew Mommy was okay now.

"You poor, poor dog." She smiled.

The information on the police radio was relayed to May, Dan and the reporters and they all headed to the park.

One of the ambulance attendants put Finnegan at Pat's feet. He curled up and fell asleep like that's all he needed.

The ambulance was readying to leave with Pat. Finnegan stayed at Pat's feet. Wanda and Carol reached the ambulance right before Pat was lifted up and into the emergency unit.

Carol picked up Finnegan and smiled at Pat. "I'll take good care of your sweet boy."

Tears were in Pat's eyes. "Thank you Carol." She added, "Thank you my friend."

Wanda said, "I may be hard of hearing, but I knew something was not right. I told Nancy, she didn't believe me."

Wanda threw a kiss to Pat. Carol cried happy tears. She waved to Pat and ruffled Finnegan's fur and said, "Good bye friend. I'll keep your boy safe. We'll see you real soon."

The ambulance took off.

Wanda said, "Imagine! She's been alive for almost three days in that casket and she still looks good."

Carol said, "Finnegan found Pat. It was meant to be. Now that he's been with me I've grown so attached to him. But this is the best news in a long time."

Larry and Scott went with Officer Bob to the Police Station and explained with a bit of trepidation how scary it was and how they knew something was just not right about Mrs. Faros. They believed they saved her life.

May walked into the police station and asked Officer Bob to release the boys; after all, they saved her mother's life. It was Larry's whistle that made the big difference.

Officer Bob took May aside and explained they were just giving the boys a serious talking to. They wanted to explain what they did was wrong even with the rescue. It saved Pat from being buried the next morning for sure, but they just wanted the boys to know the difference between right and wrong.

"We want them to understand it was wrong even though it thankfully had a happy outcome."

Mrs. Booth, Larry's mom, hurried into the police station with a frantic glare. May assured her everything was alright and that Larry was a hero. He and his friend Scott were responsible for finding that Mrs. Faros was alive in her casket and he was able to obtain the help to save her life.

May thanked them and left.

Scott's mother arrived at the police station. She saw Scott and Larry walking out of the interrogation room.

"What did you do this time Scott?"

The boys were cheered by a few people from the media when they walked out into the police station lobby.

"You won't believe it Mom, but we saved a whistling dead woman."

"You what?"

"Man, she whistled great! She was in a coffin and we saved her. We're really heroes. Ask Officer Bob. Man that was so rad."

Scott's mother said with exasperation, "What are you talking about?"

"You won't believe it. There was this dead woman... She blew a whistle that Larry put in her mouth and we saved her from being put six feet under."

May and Dan followed the ambulance to the hospital. They raced into the emergency room and May hugged her mother. They both cried.

May was still able to smell the Lysol that permeated from her mother's body.

According to the doctor in charge that evening, Pat was amazingly fine. She had had a stroke that apparently put her in a partial coma for a time, and she would need some therapy to get better mobility, but other than some bruising and a cut finger she was in pretty good health. After what she's been through she was a very lucky woman. She would have to stay in the hospital for a bit but she was in pretty good shape.

May said to herself, *who would have thought that good old Larry would have been the one person who actually had saved my mother's life?*

She told her mother that Carol was taking good care of Finnegan for the time being.

"I'll talk to you tomorrow Mom, you need to rest now."

The hospital crew was anxious to attend to Pat's immediate care, so May and Dan left.

When Michelle arrived home from the prom, she learned of her grandmother's rescue and that Larry saved her life. She was floored. She drove to Larry's house and apologized for not believing in him anymore and asked him for forgiveness.

Larry was ecstatic and felt vindicated from his antics. Michelle took him back for his... Well, in her words, 'bravery'. Larry felt he wasn't really exactly brave, so he told Michelle the true story

They broke up again. And so it goes.

Carol and Wanda ordered a pizza so they could have a much needed relaxing evening.

Wanda said in jest, "You're a firecracker. Finnegan!"

They both laughed and gave him a piece of pepperoni when the pizza arrived; as a prize.

Carol said, "I'll keep him home with me until Pat's released from the hospital."

They both agreed that Pat looked amazing for what she'd been through.

Wanda regressed back to the day she remembered hearing taps from Pat's casket.

"Bruno was on his riding mower that day. Remember? Did you hear it? I *knew* I heard her. He drowned out her tapping. Pat's gravesite will be a very memorable place now."

The next day two diggers were working feverishly, throwing dirt into the hole to fill Pat's grave back up. Splating and thudding sounds are heard.

The diggers were hired by Bruno and Blain, the owners of the cemetery, to help with an overwhelming amount of burials. But this one was the primary grave to take care of. He offered the men a cup of water from a large plastic jug he kept attached to the side of his mower. They walked over to get a drink. He asked if they'd like him to bring some donuts or something.

"No thanks, we're good. We had Mickey D's for breakfast. We just want to get done pretty quick," the younger man remarked with a smirk, "I heard this is the grave where the woman was not dead. They saved her life. We would have buried her first today if they hadn't rescued her."

Out of nowhere a yappity poodle ran up to the two men, barking and freaking out at the shoveling. One of the men threw his shovel at the dog. "Get, you little putz!"

Carol, who was walking Finnegan, heard the guy and said, "That's my friend's dog. You better not hurt him. How dare you."

Bruno turned off his mower and bent down next to the grave, calling the dog. "Hey you... Come here! I saw you the other day. We kind of got acquainted. You're the one who got crap on my hand. Come here guy!"

Finnegan stopped barking and walked over to Bruno wagging his tail. The digger who threw the shovel knelt down to try to catch the dog. Finnegan walked over to the shovel and peed on it. The digger stopped in his tracts.

Carol glared at both men. She hooked Finnegan to his leash and walked away.

Bruno said, "Oh, sorry."

EPILOGUE

After two days of healing, Pat was transferred to a rehabilitation hospital in Philadelphia where she learned to walk and worked on improving her speech.

Pat was an anomaly in the medical community. She stunned many of the doctors with how she was able to survive such an ordeal.

Her speech came back with little effort. The doctors used Pat's rehabilitation progress for research. Two months of rehab and she was able to resume her everyday life as if nothing had happened.

The press followed Pat and her progress. The paper referred to Pat as, 'The woman who cheated death'. They glorified her and how she had clung to her life.

They also acknowledged the two teenagers who had rescued her; Larry Booth and Scott Landrum. They were referred to as heroes. The Chamber of Commerce of their town of Krum gave them both a Young Hero Award for bravery. At their high school graduation ceremony they were given five hundred dollars each and special mention for going beyond the normal requirements for helping someone in distress.

May and Dan had to retrieve some of the items that Dan had packed away when he began cleaning up Pat's house the day of the funeral. Dan had already confiscated Pat's new recliner and had fallen asleep in it the day Pat was rescued.

Pat chose not to expose George to her daughter, May. After all, his story was almost unbelievable.

Two months of rehabilitation gave Pat time to evaluate who her friends are, who her enemies are, and who are now barely acquaintances, especially after the revelations she had heard during her coffin days.

Nancy Davis was barred from visiting her. Kitten attempted to visit her at her rehabilitation hospital but Pat would not even consider her for a visit. Isn't it strange how some of the confessors did not seem to want to visit her since the rescue? One wonders why.

Wanda and Carol visited Pat on several occasions filling her in on Finnegan's antics. Once they snuck him into her hospital room. That made Pat over-the-moon happy; however, they got caught and were told to never bring a dog into the hospital again.

Marc visited Pat on a daily basis. Their relationship has been growing one day at a time ever since. The shelves were finally completed.

Carol knew the day would come when Pat would want her best friend, Finnegan, to come home. It was difficult for Carol, but she could handle it now that she was able to visit Pat and Finnegan every day. They were closer than ever and rekindled their old relationship. Finnegan continued to be Carol's buddy. Now, when she came over to walk him, they visited the cemetery and got their two miles in... Every day.

THE END

THE END

www.ingramcontent.com/pod-product-compliance
Lightning Source LLC
Chambersburg PA
CBHW061603100726
47898CB00002B/502